It was slightly after midnight, a week after our birthday bash, when Alexander and I entwined our bodies, dancing to the music of Vlad and the Impalers at the Crypt. I was lost in his gaze, his chocolate eyes as irresistible to me as his red-licorice-hued lips. His brilliant smile glowed on his handsome, pale face. I felt as if we were the only couple in the club, or the world, for that matter. No one else existed to me. His pointed fangs glistened in the pulsing strobe lights, and I melted in his slow embrace. He leaned in to me, his fangs continuing to catch the flashing light. I'd been on the other end of them before, in sight and sultry temptation, but not in true bite, and each time was like it was the first—fresh, real, and tantalizingly dangerous. I imagined the bite that would take me into his world forever, and how it would feel against my neck. Would it sting like getting my ear pierced again or hurt like getting a shot, or far worse, like a bite of an animal? Or would his knife-like teeth slide in painlessly as if they were always meant to have penetrated my skin?

Kissing Coffins
Vampire Kisses 2

"Raven is exactly the kind of girl a Goth can look up to."
—*Morbid Outlook* magazine

"Readers will love this funny novel with bite!"
—*Wow* magazine

Vampireville
Vampire Kisses 3

"A fun, fast read for vampire fans."—*School Library Journal*

Dance with a Vampire
Vampire Kisses 4

"This novel, like the first three, is never short on laughs and shudders. Alexander is as romantic as ever, and Raven is still delightfully earthy. Schreiber again concocts a lively and suspenseful story that ends on a tantalizing cliff-hanger. Fans of the series will be anxious to find out whether Raven's relationship with Alexander will survive." —*VOYA*

"A good choice for Goth lovers and fans of romantic vampire stories." —*School Library Journal*

Also by Ellen Schreiber

Ellen Schreiber

Vampire Kisses 9

Immortal Hearts

 KATHERINE TEGEN BOOKS
An Imprint of HarperCollins Publishers

To my husband, Eddie,
my parents, Gary and Suzie,
and my brothers, Mark and Ben,
with hugs and vampire kisses

HarperTeen is an imprint of HarperCollins Publishers.
Katherine Tegen Books is an imprint of HarperCollins Publishers.

Vampire Kisses 9: Immortal Hearts
Copyright © 2012 by Ellen Schreiber
www.epicreads.com

Library of Congress Cataloging-in-Publication Data
Schreiber, Ellen.
Vampire kisses 9 : immortal hearts / by Ellen Schreiber. — 1st ed.
p.   cm.
Summary: The relationship of Raven and her vampire boyfriend, Alexander, is tested when
his younger sister, Stormy, comes to town.
ISBN 978-0-06-207009-8 (pbk.)
[1. Vampires—Fiction.]   I. Title.   II. Title: Vampire kisses nine.   III. Title: Immortal hearts.
PZ7.S3787Vami   2012   2011052405
[Fic]—dc23   CIP
                                                                                                       AC

18 19 LSCH 10 9 8 7 6 5 4

First paperback edition, 2013

CONTENTS

I will love you for all of eternity.

—Alexander Sterling

I was waiting for the other combat boot to drop.

My life in Dullsville had turned perfectly exciting. I was living the nightmare I'd always dreamed of—I was in love with a gorgeous vampire, and I had fabulous Underworldly friends and a hauntingly gothic nightclub where I could dance until dawn. The only thing I was missing was being an actual member of the Coffin Club—by becoming a real vampire. But if I couldn't be a vampire yet, then I would gladly enjoy the moment while I thought of new ways to convince Alexander I was truly ready to be turned.

So much had happened recently. Alexander's best friend, Sebastian, had escaped the clutches of his new girlfriend, Luna, who had been set to dig her fangs into him for eternity. Sebastian was solo now, safe and crashing out in a downtown apartment in Dullsville. Scarlet and Onyx, my two vampire ghoul friends, were still inhabiting the

Crypt and each had their mark on a guy—Scarlet had her sights set on my nemesis, Trevor Mitchell, which made me uneasy. While I didn't want to date Trevor, it was odd to see him in the company of a vampire. And Onyx had her eyes on Luna's twin brother, Jagger. And Jagger, Alexander's former nemesis, was basking in the moonlight now that his club was a hit in Dullsville. My best friend, Becky Miller, had learned Alexander's and my other friends' true vampire identities and was accepting this unexpected news as best as any mortal could. Alexander was as dreamy as ever, feeling more relaxed with a peer vampire population in this small town, and both of us were eagerly anticipating the arrival of his little sister, Athena "Stormy" Sterling.

It was slightly after midnight, a week after our birthday bash, when Alexander and I entwined our bodies, dancing to the music of Vlad and the Impalers at the Crypt. I was lost in his gaze, his chocolate eyes as irresistible to me as his red-licorice-hued lips. His brilliant smile glowed on his handsome, pale face. I felt as if we were the only couple in the club, or the world, for that matter. No one else existed to me. His pointed fangs glistened in the pulsing strobe lights, and I melted in his slow embrace. He leaned in to me, his fangs continuing to catch the flashing light. I'd been on the other end of them before, in sight and sultry temptation, but not in true bite, and each time was like it was the first—fresh, real, and tantalizingly dangerous. I imagined the bite that would take me into his world forever, and how it would feel against my neck. Would it sting like getting my ear pierced again or hurt like getting a shot, or far worse, like a bite of an animal? Or would his knife-like teeth slide in painlessly as if they were always meant to have penetrated my skin?

My blood would not be solely mine anymore but ours. I was mesmerized by my one true love and knew he was the one I'd been dreaming about to live with for an eternity. We'd cohabitate in the Underworld, strolling through cemeteries at night and cuddling in our king-sized coffin all day. I'd decorate the Mansion and run my gothic and vampy mag while Alexander painted masterworks in our attic bedroom. I'd fulfill his need for nourishment and he for me while we laughed, danced, and kissed in the darkness. Alexander's fangs slid farther down the nape of my neck until I was jarred out of my dream state. I felt myself pushed back from him, and suddenly someone was dancing between us. At first I thought a wayward dancer had bumped into us, but when I saw long, bubblegum-pink hair, I knew it was intentional. Luna swayed her lithe, fairy-like body to the morbidly slow beat and then threw her head back as if she'd just been bitten. No one was going to come between Alexander and me! I scooted myself in between them and pushed her out with all my might.

Luna sailed into another dancer and fell into his arms. I glanced over and noticed the dancer had blond hair. It was Trevor, who had once dated Luna. Scarlet wasn't going to be as gentle as I was with another girl coming between her and her man—after all, she was a real vampire. Scarlet lunged at Luna and hissed like a cat as her eyes seemed to turn blood-red. Luna ignored her and instead flashed her long, glittery pink lashes at Trevor, who was helplessly caught in her charms. Scarlet grabbed Trevor by his polo sleeve and yanked him away from the entrancing Luna. Trevor was startled by Scarlet's bold move but then smiled about the tug-of-war and possible catfight over him. He shot me a look as if to say, "See what you're missing?"

As Scarlet dragged Trevor off the dance floor, Luna appeared unfazed. She glanced around until she saw the nearest male clubster—Matt Wells, my best friend's boyfriend. Becky and Matt were jamming when Luna sidled up to Matt. He was caught off guard, and his face flushed cherry red with her sudden attention. Poor Becky seemed blindsided and didn't know what to do. I pushed my way through the crowd of dancers and pulled Luna away from my favorite couple. I'd clobber anyone who came between my best friend and her soulmate.

I gave Luna a death stare. She returned my fiery gaze, tensed her soft, pale cheeks, and bit her baby-pink lips. It must be hard for someone as beautiful as Luna to accept rejection. Until recently, rejection had been something I'd been accustomed to—it was acceptance that was new to me. However, Luna had first been rejected by Alexander and now by his best friend, Sebastian.

Luna had been a Sulky Sue since Sebastian had high-tailed it out of the Crypt when he found out the covenant ceremony he was performing with Luna was on sacred ground. If he'd bitten her as they planned, they'd be bonded together as vampire lovers for eternity. Jagger had tried to trick Sebastian into being a mate for his twin sister for a lifetime—and beyond.

Who knew what other tricks the Maxwells had up their torn sleeves? I would have to keep them in my sight.

But with Luna on the rebound and apparently moving in on our boyfriends, it was going to be impossible for any of us girls to be happy with her being solo. Everyone but Luna in relationships meant only one thing—trouble. And I knew that the guy she craved the most was my beloved Alexander.

Even though Luna was my adversary, when I gazed into her starlet-blue eyes I saw a lonely girl gazing back at me, a girl who longed for true love, just like I had before I met Alexander. And even though she was sneaky and troublesome, she, too, deserved happiness. There had to be someone out there for her to make her dreams come true—someone who wouldn't get in the way of my or my friends' love lives.

I looked away from the scowling Luna and gazed around the club hopelessly until I spotted someone familiar.

Romeo, the hot bartender from the Coffin Club, was serving bubbly liquid at the Crypt. Why hadn't I thought of him sooner? He had been right under her nose and mine. I'd never seen Romeo hanging out with one particular girl here or at the Coffin Club in Hipsterville, so I was hoping he was available for a romantic setup.

I turned back to Luna but she was gone. I couldn't see her pink hair anywhere. I pushed through the crowd and found Alexander talking to Sebastian by the club's

5

entrance. Sebastian was eyeing all the girls in the club, but one in particular had grabbed his attention since the split with Luna—Onyx. She was hanging by Jagger's side as he attended to business concerning the club.

I gave my hot-and-steamy Alexander a kiss on the cheek.

"I'll be right back," I said.

"I'll be right here." His dark locks fell over his eyes; his soft smile was mesmerizing.

I headed back to the dance floor and grabbed Becky by the sleeve.

"What's up?" she asked.

"We're on a mission."

She sighed. "Aren't we always?"

I started to guide her off the dance floor.

"But I want to dance," she whined.

Becky was growing accustomed to the club, too, along with the other students at Dullsville High. But this matter took precedence above our happiness for the night. If we didn't attempt to handle Luna's singlehood, we'd have a bigger mess on our hands later.

"This is more important than dancing," I insisted.

"But I don't want to leave Matt alone," she said as she followed me reluctantly. "I don't trust Luna. She seems to be trying to get her hands on every guy here at the club."

"I know. And we have to fix that."

"What can we do? If I leave Matt alone, she may try to come around again."

"I'll take care of that," I said.

"What are you doing?" Scarlet asked as she caught up to us.

"Trying to find a soulmate for Luna," I answered swiftly.

"Oh, good!" she said. "I'll come with you! But can we leave her alone with our guys?"

"We can in a bit," I replied to the bewildered girls.

I stormed over to the bar, where a member of Jagger's security team was watching the dance floor. The burly guard was as wide as he was tall. And he was very tall.

"Can you make sure that that pink-haired girl," I said, pointing to Luna, who was now dancing alone at the edge of the dance floor, "stays away from those three guys?" I gestured to our dates—Alexander and Sebastian, by the club's entrance, and Matt, who was hanging out by a pool table with Trevor.

"Uh . . . isn't she Jagger's sister?" he asked.

"Yes."

"Well, he's the boss." He towered over me like a concrete building.

"And I'm the customer," I insisted. "Isn't the customer always right?"

But just like a concrete building, he didn't budge.

I dug into my Hello Batty evening bag and pulled out a five. I waved it in front of him.

But the security guard didn't even look. I slipped the money into his behemoth-sized palm.

He glared at me as if I'd handed him a penny.

"Here." Becky reached into her purse and took out a

few dollars. "Our love lives depend on it."

The hulky guard couldn't help but grin as he loomed over us.

"Yes," Scarlet said, handing him another bill.

"Okay—" he finally said, "but this stays between us."

"Of course," we agreed.

"Tick a lock," I said, winding a pretend key against my dark-stained lips.

I grabbed the girls' hands and we tore through the crowd to the bar. It was impossible to find an empty stool and even harder to get Romeo's attention.

I squeezed between a preppy couple, leaned over the bar, and scooted as close to Romeo as I could. I didn't have any more money to wave. Instead I held up a white cocktail napkin. "Romeo, over here!" I called.

But Romeo was pouring and delivering as many drinks as humanly possible, even for a vampire. At this rate, we'd be waiting at the bar all night.

I couldn't wait any longer.

As he passed me by, I reached over the bar and grabbed his tattooed wrist, causing him to spill one of the drinks.

"Hey! What's going on?" he yelled.

"I'm sorry," I said. "I just need to speak with you." I knew Romeo recognized me from our previous meetings at the Coffin Club.

Romeo was handsome and a great fit for Luna, I thought. He had a tattoo of Munch's *Scream* on his bicep and Chinese characters on his wrists. His shaggy dark hair couldn't hide the countless silver studs and hoop rings in his ears. He wore a Berlin T-shirt and ripped jeans.

"Can't you see I'm busy?" He wiped off the bar and the back of his drink-soiled hand.

"It's imperative I speak with you now," I said urgently. "What do you think of Luna?" I asked him with a hopeful smile.

"Luna?" he said, half listening, as he served another drink.

"Luna Maxwell. Jagger's sister."

"I know who she is," he said as if I was bothering him.

"Well, what do you think of her?"

He turned to face me. Romeo was cute with his dark, wavy hair and intense stare. "DDG," he said.

"What's that mean?" I asked.

"Drop-dead gorgeous," he replied.

I beamed. "Then why don't you ask her out?" I asked.

"I dunno."

"I think you should. Why don't you?"

He shrugged his shoulders. "Uh . . . she's, like, sixteen."

"No—she's, like, eighteen. Maybe even nineteen."

"Really?" He perked up.

"Yes. And she's single."

"That's cool." He bounced a bit as he wiped down the bar.

"You should ask her out," I said.

"Maybe."

"I think you should. Now." I was getting impatient.

"Yes, you should," Becky repeated.

"Ditto," Scarlet added.

"Okay . . . maybe later," he finally answered.

"Later?" I asked. "We don't have time for later!"

"I can't do it now," he said as if I was crazy. "I'm working."

"How about I help out?" Scarlet whisked around the bar and joined Romeo.

"You aren't a bartender," he scoffed.

"I am now," she said.

"Who wants a cold one?" Scarlet shouted to the patrons.

Several hands raised high in the air.

But Romeo didn't move. Instead he seemed distracted by the help that Scarlet was providing him.

"I can't leave," he told me. "I could get fired."

Why did work have to come in the way of his love life—and mine? I couldn't wait until the end of his shift to get Luna hitched.

"We have to get her over to the bar," I said to Becky. At least with Scarlet helping out Romeo, he might have more time to talk to her.

"What are you doing?" Alexander asked me when he found us looking for Luna in the crowd. "I thought we were dancing."

"I just need to fix something," I said, scanning the crowd for pink pastel hair.

"Fix what?" Alexander shouted over the music. He drew me in to him. "Can't you do it later? I wait all day to see you, and the nights that we have together are cut short by you having to go home. This is our time together."

"I know," I said, feeling pulled in two directions. I didn't want to be apart from Alexander any more than was forced on us by the sun. "But you'll have to trust me on this one." If Luna wasn't in a romantic relationship, then the time I was apart from Alexander would be even harder for me since I knew she'd still be after him.

I reached up and gave him a quick peck on his tender lips. "I won't be but a moment. I promise."

Alexander shook his head, and Sebastian asked, "What's up?"

"Just Raven getting into another one of her messes, I'm sure," Alexander said with a chuckle.

I spotted pink hair out among the blondes and brunettes; Becky, Onyx, and I raced over.

I took Luna aside while my friends hung behind me.

"I think Romeo wants to talk to you," I said in as sweet a voice as I could to my adversary. "He said he really likes you."

"Romeo?" she asked skeptically.

"Yes, don't you think he's hot?" I asked as if it were fact.

"He's the bartender," she said flatly.

"Yes. The *hot* bartender."

Onyx and Becky nodded their heads enthusiastically.

"I guess." Luna couldn't be bothered with my small talk and tapped her fuchsia Mary Janes to the music.

"Haven't you noticed him before?" I asked.

"Uh . . . yes. He works for Jagger."

"I know. So what do you think of him?" I inquired eagerly.

She just shrugged her shoulders.

I didn't know much about Romeo except that he was a bartender and that he was nice. In fact, I didn't even know if he was a vampire, but I assumed that, because he worked at the Coffin Club and was in Jagger's inner circle, he must be. I wasn't sure what else to tell her, other than what I'd seen of him.

"He's really worldly," I said, recalling his T-shirt.

"How do you know that?" she asked.

"He's been to Berlin. He loves to travel."

"So? I've been there, too."

"You have? See, you already have things in common. There aren't many guys here who have been to Chicago, much less Berlin."

"I guess that's cool," she said with halfhearted interest.

Becky and Onyx nodded again.

"And he loves art," I added, remembering his tattoo. "He'll take you to the greatest museums."

"He's an artist, too?"

"I think so," I fibbed. "Maybe he can use you as a model for a painting," I suggested.

"He sounds just like Alexander," Becky interjected.

I was ready to stomp on my friend's foot, but Luna's sparkly pink-lashed eyes lit up like a crystal.

That was all Luna needed to know. She sailed over to the bar, and a guy offered her his stool.

She hopped on it, threw back her long pink hair, and leaned her elbows on the bar.

"What can I get you?" Romeo asked.

It was magic when their eyes locked.

"Well, that depends," Luna said in a sultry voice. "What's on the menu?"

"Romeo, I need your help!" Scarlet called. She was up to her elbows in drink orders.

Oh no! I'd finally made a love connection for Luna that didn't involve any of my or my friends' guys, and it was going to be messed up within seconds.

"Stay where you are!" I said to Romeo. "We'll help her."

Becky followed me as we raced behind the bar.

"I don't know the first thing about making drinks," Becky said, overwhelmed with our new mission.

"I don't, either. But since there isn't alcohol in them, it can't be that hard."

"I'm not so sure. . . ." Becky whimpered.

"Just stick an umbrella in it," I said. "It's that easy."

I found bartending wasn't as easy as adding cute garnishes to frosted glasses. I had to take back as many drinks as I served, and Scarlet was taking in all the tips. Becky and I owed more than we came with, and I hadn't had a chance yet to get back to Alexander.

Alexander finally found us at the bar, exhausted and spent.

"What are you doing here?" he asked, shocked. He and

Sebastian sat down on two empty stools. I was pouring a cola from the soda gun; my hair was falling in my face and my charcoal-colored eyeliner was smearing in the heat.

"What would you like?" I asked him. "How about a Serial Killer?"

"We were looking everywhere for you," he said, concerned. "You didn't answer your phone."

"Oh, sorry! I didn't hear it ring," I apologized. "It must be in my purse. I had no idea how hard this job can be. There are three of us here, and we still can't keep up."

"Why isn't Romeo working?" Sebastian asked.

"He is. Look," I said. Romeo and Luna were lost in each other's gaze. "Isn't that sweet?"

"That's what this is all about?" Alexander said, scrutinizing them.

"I'm glad she has her fangs on someone else," Sebastian said, his blond dreads bobbing as he turned her way. "That girl is cook-a-loo—!"

"She is not," I chimed in. "Well, sort of. I mean, she wanted you," I said to Alexander, "and then you," I said to Sebastian. "And you both rejected her at the altar. How should she feel?"

Both guys thought for a moment before Alexander spoke. "What do you know about Romeo?" he asked me as I wiped off my hands with the bar rag.

"I know he isn't you. And to me that's all he has to be. Besides, why are you worried about who she dates?"

Alexander shot me a look. "I just want you to be matchmaking for the right reason."

"I am," I replied. "I want her to be happy so she doesn't try to steal you away. I think that is the best reason one could have."

"Why would she steal me away?" He leaned in close and took my hand. "Don't I have a choice in this? Don't you trust me?" he asked.

I trusted a lot of things—I was confident with my style, taste, and opinions. And I was secure with my relationship with Alexander. However, Luna, who was sneaky to say the least, had known Alexander before I did and had grown up with his family in Romania. And now that she was inhabiting Dullsville and living in the Crypt, which was only a few miles away from the Mansion, she was too close for comfort. I didn't trust either her or her brother, and without Sebastian as the object of her romantic attentions she would surely aim her affection toward my true love, Alexander, once again.

"I don't trust *her*," I said.

He pushed my sweaty hair away from my face and took the drink from my hand and placed it on the bar.

"You did all that so we could be together?" he asked, massaging my cola-sticky hand.

"Uh-huh."

"That might be one of the sweetest things in the world," he said. "But don't worry—it will take more than pink eyelashes to keep me away from you."

"I still can't believe Alexander is a real vampire," Becky said the following day at Evans Park. We met at the swings, our usual outdoor hangout. No one was around, and we could talk freely about the Underworld.

Becky had a revulsion to my favorite haunts—cemeteries—and the swings always brought back memories of childhood. And I loved that swinging as high as I could gave me the closest feeling I ever had to flying.

"It's really hard to imagine that it is true," she continued, trying to keep up with me.

"I know," I shouted proudly. "And there's more. Jagger and Luna. Scarlet and Onyx. And Romeo . . ."

"And Sebastian?" she asked.

"Yes. Cool, isn't it? And to think they are all living here in Dullsville."

"It is so overwhelming. But most of all, Alexander."

Becky was full of questions about the Underworld. And even if I'd already answered them, she wanted me to tell her again.

Becky dragged her white Keds into the dirt, and I followed suit with my untied combat boots. "When did you know?" she asked as I caught my breath. "I mean really know, like I do now?"

"I suspected when I first met him—especially because the people around town were saying his family were vampires. But I didn't really know for certain until I *didn't* see his reflection in Ruby's compact mirror."

"And you didn't tell me," she said with a sad longing.

"I wanted to!" I responded sincerely.

"I know it must have been hard. I'd have to tell you something like that immediately."

I'd always felt guilty that I hadn't blabbed the vampire news to my friend then. But I also had an obligation to Alexander. And the more I grew to know him, the more the sense of obligation was stronger.

"I wanted to every time I saw you," I defended. "I even tried once—"

"I know you did. I guess I just wasn't ready to hear it."

"And now you are," I said.

"It's hard for me not to want to tell everyone, too. My parents . . ."

"But you know you can't!" I insisted. "If word gets out, they'll all be run out of town. And that includes Alexander."

"I know. But it's *so* hard. That's why I have to talk about it with you."

"Have you told Matt?" I asked.

She appeared shocked, as if I'd caught her stealing candy. "You said I could!"

"I know. I couldn't imagine you keeping it from him, and for some reason he doesn't seem to have loose lips."

"Well, I told him."

"Did he freak out?"

"Yes. I still don't think he believes me. But I think the fact that I knew made me seem more worldly or something to him."

"That's cool."

"I thought so, too." Becky grinned. "So what's it really like dating a vampire? You have to wait all day to see Alexander?"

"Yes."

"Like now?"

"Uh-huh."

"Until the sun sets?" she asked, looking at the bright sky.

I nodded.

"Isn't that awful? I can see Matt at school *and* on the weekend. How can you take it? You are missing so much."

"Thanks for reminding me," I said sarcastically.

"I just mean . . ."

"I know. That part is a drag." It was one of the many reasons I longed to become a vampire—so Alexander and I could be together full-time. "But since I like the night-time and sleep through most days when I can, it's really the perfect fit," I told her.

"Does he sleep in a coffin?" she asked.

"Yes."

"Have you seen it?"

"Yes.

"Is it in a dungeon?"

"No, in a small room off of his bedroom."

"Have you been inside it?"

"Yes."

"Oooh. I bet you loved it!"

"I did!"

"Do you think . . . I could see it sometime?"

"I'm sure you can."

"I can't imagine Alexander sleeping in a coffin. I mean, I can—he is different, in a good way. But Matt—everything is pretty normal about him. I can't imagine what I'd do if I went to his room and found him sleeping in a casket."

"I know exactly what you'd do. Faint!"

Her cheeks flushed as we both laughed. "But for you," she began, "isn't it a dream come true for you really, to be dating a vampire?"

"It is, Becky. It is. And I'm so happy that we can finally talk about it. I've been dying to tell you for ages."

"And does he really drink . . . ?"

I nodded eagerly as she cringed.

"And you still want to become one?"

I nodded again.

"Does he try to bite you?"

"No, but I wish he would."

She shook her head at me. "So do you think it will happen?" she asked, slightly terrified, clinging to the swing's metal chain link.

I was quiet for a moment.

She hung on for my answer.

"I don't know."

"What do you mean, you don't know?"

"It takes *two* for me to become a vampire. I can't do it alone. I need Alexander."

"Of course. Isn't he willing?"

"He wants to protect me from his world. He thinks I might hate it. I understand his struggle. It's a big decision to make for someone else."

"That *is* a big decision."

And something I wanted so badly to happen. "But he did take my blood," I confessed proudly. This was big news, and I felt like I'd burst with joy to finally be sharing it with my best friend.

"You are kidding!"

"No!" I exclaimed. "I had a cut—just like you did that night when you fell and Sebastian took . . ."

"What?"

Then I realized. Becky hadn't known what Sebastian had done that night. "Oh . . . nothing."

"No. What were you going to say?" she pressed.

"Uh . . . it's not important."

"You have to tell me. What do you mean, that night I fell?"

"Uh . . . you skinned your knee."

"I know—I remember that. And Sebastian helped me when I began to bleed." Her eyes grew wide as she remembered. "Oh no! Then you pushed him away. I thought it was odd then—that you struggled with him when he was trying to help me. But now that I know . . . Did he bite me? Did Sebastian bite me? Am I going to be a . . . ?"

"No, calm down. He wiped off your blood from your knee. That's all."

"Why would he do that?" she wondered. "There's more, isn't there?"

"Not really. He didn't bite you. That's all you need to know."

"But he wiped it off. I remember."

"Yes, he did."

"But what did he do with the blood?" she asked, trying to remember. Then she looked at me as if she already knew the answer.

I reluctantly nodded, recalling how he put his blood-stained finger to his mouth.

"Oh, gross!" She covered her ears. "I don't want to hear."

"You just told me you want to know everything."

"I didn't need to know *that* part. I feel woozy." Then, suddenly, she clutched my shirt. "Will I turn into a vampire?" she asked desperately.

"No. You are no more a vampire than I am."

"Are you sure?"

"Dead sure."

My best friend sighed with relief.

"No, you have to be bitten for that to happen," I said with a sigh of my own. But there was something I wasn't sure she knew. Something I wanted to have happen to me. "And if the vampire bites another on sacred ground, then they are bonded together for eternity," I said. "Isn't that romantic?"

"Uh . . . yes. I guess," she said uneasily. "But what is sacred ground?"

"A burial site. A cemetery. Or a tomb. But Alexander took my blood, too," I said, not wanting to feel left out of the drama. "Not on sacred ground, but like Sebastian did to you. Only it was really magical for us."

"Well, it would be to you, but to me, it's completely gross. I think I will stick with Matt. Fortunately for me the only thing he likes to drink is Gatorade."

We both laughed at the extraordinary situation that was now our reality.

"But do you still want to be a vampire now that you know the truth?" Becky asked.

"I've known for a while."

"I know. But seeing them interact—their lifestyle and their needs. Do you really want to be one like you've always wanted to before?"

"Yes. More so than ever."

She nervously twisted the ends of her hair and took a moment to process my answer.

"Would we still be able to be best friends?" Becky seemed seriously worried.

"Why not?"

"Because if you are a vampire . . . you wouldn't be going to school anymore. I'd miss you in classes, lunch, and after school. I'd only be able to see you a few hours in the evenings. Who would I talk to at school?"

"Matt."

"But *you* are my best friend."

"I would still be your best friend. Nothing will change that."

"I need girl time. I can't imagine going to school without you."

Her words hit me like a dagger in my heart. I didn't want to hurt Becky by becoming what I wanted to be. I'd always thought about the positives of being a vampire, with one of the best being that I wouldn't have to go to school during the day anymore. But I hadn't thought about the downside—not seeing my best friend, Becky, every day.

"Well, we don't have to worry about that now." I tried to ease her mind. "Alexander isn't planning on turning me any time soon—at least not that I know of."

"It must be hard for him, being a vampire and loving a human."

"I think it is. He tells me so."

"Maybe that's why you two get along so well. You both understand and crave the other's world."

I leaned back in my swing. "Yes. I crave it even more since I met Alexander. I feel like I'm only a step away."

"Really. So soon?"

"I don't know. I just want it so bad."

"We only have one more year in school before college,"

she said. "I'm hoping you'll at least wait until then?"

I could feel the sense of dread coming from Becky regarding this change. It could have simply been college—but this matter was also about a life change. Becky and I had been best friends since third grade. Our friendship wasn't something either one of us was prepared to give up—and I had truly never thought about that when I envisioned being a vampire.

"I'd die without you, Raven," she burst out, hopping off her swing.

"Me too, Becky," I said, following after her. "Nothing will keep us apart."

"Not college—" she urged.

"Or the Underworld," I added. I was surprised I said it. It was new to me to be able to share the secret I'd been holding about Alexander, the Maxwells, and Sebastian.

Her smooth forehead wrinkled in shock. She was still getting used to the idea of the new reality herself.

"Besides, it isn't something we have to deal with now." I tried to reassure her. "Alexander hasn't walked me down the cemetery aisle yet, has he? And neither one of us has really talked about college."

"We'll agree to go to the same one, then. You and me and Matt and Alexander."

"Duh!" I said. I didn't imagine Becky was planning to go to some fancy-schmancy college with outrageous tuition and a billion miles from Dullsville.

"Even if we have to meet in night classes," she added.

"Agreed!" I put my arm around her shoulder.

"But what if you don't wait until then?" she asked. "Alexander gave you that eternity ring." She pointed to my ring finger.

I never took off the glistening ring with a black diamond heart in the center. Not even in the shower or when I slept.

"Yes . . . but . . ."

"I see the way Alexander looks at you. Now that I know the truth, I know what he is thinking. I thought it was just his European charisma." She laughed. "But it's not, Raven. He wants you in a way that is not . . ."

"Human?" I asked.

She nodded her head.

I felt a huge beam of warm energy flood through me. But what I took as a compliment from Becky was something she meant as a big concern.

Though I felt melancholy about any type of change that led my best friend and me to being apart even for a minute, I did like the reassurance from someone else that Alexander craved me in a way that only a vampire could.

"It will be okay, Becky," I said. "No matter what happens between Alexander and me, you and I will always be best friends. You can count on that forever."

Becky and I gave each other a quick hug before heading off to her truck to get some coffee.

I was ready for an eternity with my true love, but not an eternity apart from my best friend.

"I saw how quickly you yanked Luna off of me at the Crypt," Trevor said to me in the hallway the following day at school. "The lengths you go to, just to keep girls away from me."

"I was helping out Scarlet, not you. And on second thought, maybe I should have *saved* Scarlet by letting Luna paw on you instead."

He grinned mischievously. His devilish nature couldn't mask his attractiveness. I felt ensnared by his gaze.

He fingered his blond locks and leaned in to me, then whispered, "It's so clear who you'd really prefer to be your real boyfriend, and that's me."

"When will you get over your delusions?" I asked. "I'm not even sure what Scarlet sees in you," I said.

Trevor inched even closer, his green eyes piercing through me. "But I think you do. I think you always have. Do you know why I like Scarlet?"

"Because she breathes?"

He smiled churlishly, his milky white teeth beaming. "Because she reminds me of you. When I am kissing her I imagine that I'm kissing you."

I was taken aback. Trevor never knew when to stop. "Don't be cruel! She's my friend."

"Which is worse?" he asked, getting in my face. "That I kiss her and think of you? Or that when I'm on the end of her succulent lips, that I might *not* be thinking of you?"

Trevor was a tease. Of course I didn't want him to use Scarlet, and I didn't want him to like me, either. But was I being honest with myself when there was a tiny piece of me that got a rise out of Trevor's torment? Or was it just something I'd grown accustomed to all my life?

Trevor drew me in to him. "How about now I'll kiss you and you can see for yourself who I am thinking of?"

I pushed against him as hard as I could, my black nails standing out against his yellow polo shirt. I knew he wasn't going to force a kiss on me, but his embrace told me he got a kick out of my trying to squirm away from him.

For a moment, I thought about kissing him back, giving him the biggest shock of his life. But I remembered Alexander. And his lips were the only ones I wanted to be on the end of—regardless of how much I wanted to torment my nemesis.

"I can spit," I told him instead.

Trevor immediately released me and jumped away. "I'd say 'You wouldn't dare,' but I know *you* would."

"Don't tempt me," I said, adjusting my dress.

"Halloween is coming," he said as if it was a warning. "Jagger is planning to have a spectacular event down at the Crypt. Luna, Scarlet, all the girls will be there with me. Too bad you won't be."

How did Trevor always know more about the vampires' plans than I did?

"I'll be there. With Alexander," I charged back.

"What horrible monster will you come as this year?" he asked. "Yourself?"

I really loathed Trevor. No matter how hard I tried, he always seemed to be one step ahead of me.

"I'll be the one dressed as your psychiatrist," I said, and headed off for class.

* * *

I felt extra groggy when I awoke in Alexander's coffin. I lazily rolled over and snuggled up close to him, hoping to doze back to sleep. He caressed my hair and I felt amazingly at peace in his embrace.

"Good morning, Monster Girl!" I heard a familiar voice say.

Then a cell phone was turned on, illuminating the inside of the casket, and I saw green eyes staring back at me. How did I get in a coffin with Trevor Mitchell? Where was Alexander? What was happening?

I tried to break open the coffin lid, but it wouldn't budge. I pushed against it with my feet as hard as I could.

"Let me out!" I screamed. "Let me out!"

"It's too late," my nemesis said. "We are here together for eternity."

His hand crept across my neck as if it was marking his territory.

I smacked it away. "Let go!" I yelled. "Alexander!"

"Isn't this what you wanted?" Trevor asked.

"Not with you! Never with you!"

"But I thought it was me all along. When you were little, didn't you try to get me to bite you so I could turn you into a vampire? It's what you always wanted, Raven."

"Let me out!"

I screamed and kicked and pleaded. I could feel my nails scraping against the wooden casket lid. I was sure my fingers were dripping with blood.

"Raven!" I heard a girl's voice say.

I awoke with my fingers digging into my school desk.

Becky was nudging me in the side.

I tried to hide my embarrassment as all my classmates stared at me. I was used to stares—but this time I felt like an idiot. I glanced around, and one particular student was grinning back at me: Trevor. I felt like somehow he'd just witnessed my whole dream, too. Beads of sweat peppered my brow, and I wiped my perspiring hands on my black tights.

Mr. Simmons glared at me and shook his head.

"Miss Madison," he said in a teacherly voice. "I'd give you a detention, but I'm afraid you'd sleep through that as well."

For the first time in high school, I agreed with one of my teachers.

That night at the Crypt, I was anxious to see what information I could get on Jagger's Halloween haunted house plans and how Luna and Romeo's relationship was percolating.

Alexander drove me to the club, and when I entered, the new lovebats were cuddling next to the bar. Luna was stroking Romeo's wavy hair and flashing her butterfly lashes. When he broke away to serve a drink, she blew kisses at him.

I was really impressed with how quickly her affections had turned to Romeo. But I couldn't blame her. He was really cute, and being older made him alluring, too.

When Luna caught sight of me, she waved me over. She was sitting at the bar in a tattered black shirt, a coral-colored flirty skirt, and chunky Doc Martens with pink laces.

I was shocked and checked around to make sure I really was the object of her attention. She waved again, as if it were obvious we were old friends; Alexander hung by Sebastian while I headed to the bar.

She spun around on the barstool. "Isn't Romeo dreamy?" Luna stopped and pressed close to me as if she wanted to literally rub her words in my face.

"Uh . . . yes," I agreed.

"And he's *so* mature. Not like these *younger* guys." I knew who she meant and who that comment was directed toward: Alexander. Funny, these younger guys had been fine with her before as she tried to date most of them.

"Well, I think some guys here are really mature," I said defensively.

She didn't have time for my response and threw her long pink locks behind her. "Romeo loves so many things," she explained. "And I'm one of them!"

"That's great." I was really excited for Luna; after all, I was the one who set her up with Romeo, so naturally I wanted them to hit it off. But Luna had a way of turning everything good into something adversarial. Instead of letting me find joy in her newfound happiness, she was tormenting me.

Luna twirled a piece of her Barbie-pink hair around her snow-white fingers. "He said he always liked me but thought I was younger than I am. I think it's because of my smooth skin."

"Yes, that's probably it." I did my best not to roll my eyes.

"And he knows what he wants out of life. He isn't floundering around like the guys in this town—freaking out at commitments. Romeo is mature—he's not a total commitment-phobe, unlike some people around here."

I did my best not to yank her off the barstool.

"I'm so happy you *finally* found someone," I said like a thrilled parent.

Luna stopped twirling her hair. Her smile stiffened, and I knew she didn't like my crack.

"Well, I'll have you know, we talked all last night about our future—that is, when we weren't making out. Romeo wants to take me downstairs to the covenant altar, bite me, and bond our lives together for eternity. Isn't that dreamy?" She batted her eyelashes purposefully.

My heart dropped. How could they make *that* decision so quickly? It had only been a few days—nights, in their case. Or was this one of Luna's lies to get me jealous? Or even worse, was this another Maxwell ploy, like it had been with Sebastian, to be bonded without his knowledge? I assumed that Romeo had heard by now that the downstairs club was built right over a Civil War burial site. I wasn't sure if this idea was something real or something Luna made up to spite me.

Instead of being mad, I decided to try the opposite approach.

"I'm the one that fixed you up, remember? I'm so

happy that you found love so quickly."

"Oh yeah. That's right," she said as if she was disappointed it had been me who was the one who had found her true-love-for-the-moment. Her scowl brightened, and she gushed like a bride. "Then I have you to thank," she said. "You can be my bridesmaid!"

She gave me a fake girlie hug—the kind that the popular girls at Dullsville High give when they greet each other at their lockers, then talk behind one another's backs.

The last thing I wanted was for Luna to beat me to the covenant altar. In Romania, fine. But here in Dullsville? I was first in line. And to be her bridesmaid? Forget it. I wasn't even going to attend!

The Maxwell twins were known for their tricks. It wasn't too long ago that Jagger and Luna tried to trick Sebastian into bonding with her for eternity. Was Romeo the next one to be taken to the sacred altar unknowingly? That wasn't part of my plan when I had arranged for them to date.

"Does he even know he's the groom?" I charged. "You do have a history of leaving important information out when taking your boyfriends to a covenant altar. Like the fact that it's on sacred ground."

"He knows. Romeo knows all about the Crypt. And about the burial sites below the Covenant. It was his idea to be bonded, not mine," she said, triumphantly flipping her nose at me. "Can you say the same about your boyfriend?"

Her words stung me. Always giving me a jab about

Alexander and my relationship. And she was diverting me from the task at hand.

If Romeo really did want to be with Luna, perhaps it was a good thing. The more she knew that it made me jealous, the faster she'd be to get hitched. Maybe I was thinking about this in the wrong way. The sooner Luna was locked and loaded to some guy, the sooner I could breathe easy that she wouldn't be so stuck on Alexander. So what was there not to like about this plan?

"Sure," I said. "You should do it soon! Before he gets away. You name the time, and we'll go shopping for dresses."

"Well . . ."

"And even though you just met him, you'll have all of eternity to find out if you guys made the right decision so quickly."

Just then, I spotted Jagger coming up from downstairs. "Let's go talk to your brother about the good news," I continued. "We'll make a huge affair for you. We can invite the whole town."

Suddenly Luna's waxlike face flushed cherry red, and her pink lips tensed. She wanted me to be mopey and in a jealous frenzy about her fast-moving relationship and obviously didn't like my enthusiasm.

"I'm not so sure . . ." she said, her bright tone darkening.

"Yeah, this will be great," I went on. "Alexander can be one of Romeo's groomsmen!"

That image hit her hard. Alexander standing on the altar with her but not being the one she was bonding with for eternity. I thought she might explode.

"What?" she said. "Are you nuts? We just started dating!" She hopped off the stool and glared her baby-blue eyes at me. "Gosh, you are so immature!" She threw her hair back again and left me standing alone by the empty stool.

I spun the stool around in victory. I guess I didn't have to worry about Luna's covenant plans for now. I breathed a sigh of relief. Everything with her was tied up for a while into a nice pink-and-black-skull bow, and I could go back to normal—whatever "normal" meant.

I was starting to leave to join Scarlet and Onyx when someone grabbed my shirtsleeve. I turned back to find Luna suddenly by my side.

"By the way," she said, "I can't wait until Stormy comes here. It's as if the puzzle will be completed. She's like family to me, you know."

My heart dropped. Like family to Luna? They were close—that close?

"Uh . . . you know Stormy?"

"Know her? I practically raised her. I was her babysitter," Luna exclaimed as if I should have known. "We are like sisters. I guess you couldn't know," she continued. "You haven't even *met* her."

Now *my* lips were tensing. How did Luna even know Stormy was coming to town? And why was she so excited?

"She's coming to visit Alexander," I said emphatically.

"I know," she said, almost squealing. "I can't wait!"

This was something I hadn't even imagined. I knew Alexander had been in an arranged covenant with Luna—which he rejected—but I wasn't aware of Luna's history with Alexander's sister.

"I thought you were mortal then," I said. "Wouldn't it be hard to sit for her when she's up all night and you're not?" I was hoping she was lying.

"It was. But I'd stay up all night with her until the Sterlings got home. I was her favorite sitter. I can't wait to see her again!"

Jealousy seared through me, this time in a big way. Not only did Luna know about a sister that Alexander had who I'd only recently learned about—but she had already had a relationship with her. I could only wonder what Luna was like as a babysitter. She had to be the coolest one ever. Making Count Chocula treats, telling ghost stories instead of bedtime stores, and sliding down banisters like witches on broomsticks.

Not like my sitters, who mostly never returned after one night of playing with the shaven-head dolls in my Barbie Nightmare House and cooking spider-shaped cakes in my Easy-Bake Oven.

Luna had everything I wanted—except Alexander—and though he was the one thing that mattered most to me, she still wound up getting under my temporary-tattooed, bone-white skin.

"She gets in soon," she went on. "I can't wait to have

her here at the Crypt. She'll die when she sees it!"

Then she let go of my sleeve. Luna whirled away from me, and I could hear her laughing as she slipped behind the bar and cozied up with Romeo.

Luna was evil. I wanted to be the one to bring Stormy to the Crypt, and Luna already had plans for that. How could I compete with her? I normally wasn't jealous of others—there wasn't much that I desired from people in Dullsville. But Luna had it all, and even though I had one thing she wanted—Alexander—she somehow managed to make her life's mission to see to it that I was the loser. And if I let her, she would do just that.

"Where have you been?" Scarlet asked when I caught up to the girls.

"Talking to Luna," I answered through gritted teeth. I couldn't hide my frustration.

"What about?" Becky asked. "You seem tense."

"Yes, are you okay?" Onyx asked sweetly.

"Just about Romeo," I said. "She's all into him, which is great. Hopefully this is for real this time."

Becky received this news with a smile. But then she asked, "So why do you look angry? This is what we wanted."

"I know," I said. "But she just likes to throw all her relationships in my face. It gets old."

"Well, you have the one she really wants," Scarlet said. "So don't give her another thought."

I was comforted by my friend's reassurance, but I still was bugged about Luna having such a strong relationship with Stormy before I'd even gotten the chance to meet her. When I saw Trevor walk into the club, another foe's taunts flashed before me.

"Did you hear that Jagger is planning on having a Halloween bash?" I asked them suddenly.

"No," Scarlet replied. She put her hands on her hips as if she, too, was surprised to have not been involved in the business-minded Maxwells' plans.

But Onyx didn't answer.

"You know something?" Scarlet asked her friend.

"Well . . ." Onyx responded softly.

"Spill it," Scarlet ordered.

"I think he's going to turn the Crypt into a haunted house for Halloween."

"That's awesome!" I said.

"I can't wait!" Becky said.

"That will be the greatest, ever," I added.

"I overheard him talking," Onyx said. "He's still working on the plans."

"But why didn't he tell us?" Scarlet said. "What's the big secret?" Just then Sebastian approached us, his blond dreadlocks bouncing with every step.

"Can I have this dance?" he said to Onyx, like a gentleman.

Scarlet, Becky, and I were surprised by Sebastian's invitation. He knew Onyx was smitten with Jagger, but since Sebastian had been tricked by the Maxwells, I assumed he didn't care.

No one was more surprised than Onyx. "I was waiting for . . ." she began.

"Go ahead," Scarlet said, gently pushing her toward him. "It's time you branch out."

Onyx reluctantly obliged, and she and Sebastian rocked together in the middle of the dance floor.

"If Jagger keeps holding secrets from us," Scarlet said, "then it's time for us to find a new Jagger."

My blood was boiling when I finally found Alexander by the bar.

"What's wrong?" he asked. "Where is that beautiful smile?"

I tried focusing my energy on Alexander, but I couldn't help but think of the Maxwells and how they got on my nerves.

"Well, Jagger is going to have a haunted house and he told Trevor and not us, and Luna is going to bring Stormy here before I can."

"Whoa. Slow down," Alexander said. His calming tone melted me, but I was still frazzled. "What about Jagger?"

"For Halloween, he is going to have a haunted house here at the Crypt. I found out from the girls at the club. And Trevor knew something was up before we did. He told me Jagger was going to have a 'spectacular event' for Halloween."

"Trevor?"

"Yes."

"Oh." Alexander looked away.

"What's wrong?" I asked.

"Nothing . . ." But his voice was shallow and distant.

"Please tell me."

"I don't know. . . . It's just annoying that he's the one that gets to see you all day when it should be me."

"Believe me, you are the only one I've ever wanted to see," I tried to reassure him.

"I know. But it's one of the things I miss by being a vampire."

I felt for him. Alexander experienced the same longing I did for him by not being able to completely share our worlds.

"I hate it, too. I wish you could be by my side at school. Hang out by our lockers. Sneak off for a kiss. But then again, you wouldn't be you." I gave him a soft smile.

"So, Trevor knows first," Alexander said. "Is that really a big deal?"

"Yes," I insisted. I wanted to be the first to have any new Crypt information, and I thought we deserved to be in Jagger's inner circle. "We hang out here all the time. We should know everything. And that means Jagger is still keeping secrets from us. What else does he have planned?"

"But a haunted house isn't something that we need to know about," he said in Jagger's defense.

"Are you serious?"

"Yes," he went on, pushing his dark locks away from

his face. "It's his right, really. If he wants us to know, he can tell. If not, no big deal. It's just a haunted house."

Just a haunted house? I thought. This was a haunted house dreamed up by a living, breathing vampire. And not being in on the idea from the beginning made the news really sting, especially when Trevor knew before me.

"Now what's this about Luna and Stormy?" Alexander went on.

"Luna is shoving it in my face that she and Stormy are like sisters. And I haven't even met her." I folded my arms like a child.

"Stormy's not here yet," Alexander said. "Why are you worrying about this now?"

"Luna seems to think she gets to bring Stormy to the Crypt, not us. Not me."

I felt like I was in first grade. I was getting all wound up over something Luna might or might not do. But just the thought and her goading me was enough to make steam rise from my multipierced ears.

"How about this?" Alexander said. "Stormy's *my* sister, and *I'll* bring her here. And since you are my girlfriend, you'll be coming with us. Luna will see her in due time. I want you and Stormy to get a chance to hang out. And I know Stormy will want that as well."

"Thank you!" I flung my arms around Alexander. I wanted to be a part of his family, and I didn't want anyone to come between us—especially someone as wicked as Luna Maxwell.

* * *

For the rest of the night I was buzzing. When I wasn't dancing with Alexander, I was hanging with Becky and my vampire ghoul friends. It was interesting to see Luna and Romeo together, whether it was for spite or if she truly found him irresistible. Sebastian seemed to be in heaven dancing with Onyx, and I was happy to find him having such a good time.

Jagger finally came up from his office downstairs and noticed Sebastian and Onyx on the dance floor together. His ashen face flushed as blood-red as the dyed tips of his white hair. Jagger immediately stormed over to Sebastian and wedged himself between the two.

"What's up, dude?" Sebastian asked, surprised.

"Can't find your own date, *dude*?" Jagger charged.

Sebastian wasn't deterred. He wasn't a menacing figure, but he wasn't one to be pushed around, either.

"Yes I can, and she's right here," he replied, continuing to dance.

"I can have you removed from the club," Jagger said, snapping his black-fingernailed fingers, "like that." The tension was mounting, and I worried it was going to break out into a fight.

Scarlet must have overheard the commotion because she bravely stepped in.

"I think Onyx can choose for herself," she said to Jagger defiantly.

Onyx looked at all of us and got flustered. For a moment she stood speechless, then fled the dance floor.

Scarlet hurried after her. Alexander came to Sebastian's side and pulled him away from Jagger and off toward the bar, diffusing the tension between the two vampires.

Jagger put his hands on his hips, shook his head, then disappeared the other way. I grabbed Becky and we found Scarlet and Onyx talking in the restroom.

"I'm not sure what to do," Onyx said, patting her face with a paper towel. "I really like Jagger."

There was only one mirror on the wall for the mortal attendees. The vampire girls were standing on the other side of the room so as not to raise suspicions about any absent reflections.

"But I think Sebastian is cool, too. I love his dread-locks," Onyx continued, "and he is so laid back and kind where Jagger seems . . ."

"Dangerous?" I prompted.

"Yes." Onyx turned to me, surprised by my answer.

"He is," I said. But wasn't that why Jagger was appealing? He did ooze sex appeal and power, and that tinge of danger was just the right kind of edginess that made him attractive.

"But Sebastian is so fun," Onyx went on. "He's really sweet, and I like that he loves to just hang out."

"Yes, Matt is really laid back, too," Becky said. "That makes it really nice."

I thought about Alexander, who was so exciting to be with, too, no matter what we did.

"Well, I love the danger," Scarlet chimed in. "Trevor seems so clean cut, but he does have this dark edge. He's so conservative, but it's really like he should be wearing chains and studded earrings."

"So you like his dark side?" Becky asked. "I don't like that side of him."

But I knew what Scarlet was referring to. She found the side of Trevor that was conniving and menacing attractive.

"Yes," Scarlet wailed. "And that he is mega-hot!" They all giggled, but I rolled my eyes.

"That's why I'm confused," Onyx said. "I like that Sebastian is spontaneous, but I also like that Jagger is so headstrong and focused on his clubs. It's really sexy."

"Matt is passionate about soccer. It is really cool to date someone who has a passion. I can see why you like that in Jagger," Becky said.

Alexander was passionate about his art. It was one of the traits that made him so alluring. I agreed that their interests did make our guys that much more dreamy.

"Well, Trevor is passionate, too." Scarlet paused and looked to me. I wasn't sure what she was going to say next, but I sensed she was referring to me. "Soccer, too," she eventually said. "Trevor has so many layers to him."

Yes, I thought. *You peel back the layers of a jerk and find a bigger jerk.*

Everything just felt right with Alexander. I could make a list of the things I liked about him, but there was something deeper to it that I couldn't quite put into words but that let me know he was the one. Our relationship just felt like heaven.

"You don't have to make a decision this minute," Scarlet said. "For now, *we'll* dance together."

"Yes, let them fight for you," Becky said like an old pro in the romantic game. "It can be very exciting."

4

Shopping for a Ghoul

T he following evening, Alexander and I were making our way down the attic stairs of the Mansion when we saw Jameson entering one of the vacant bedrooms on the second floor.

"Just getting it ready for Miss Athena's arrival," Alexander's butler said.

I was thrilled that the time was getting closer for Stormy to arrive in Dullsville. But the bedroom that Jameson was readying was bare except for a small dresser, making it feel cold and lonely. It didn't look comforting for a younger sibling to inhabit, and I was wondering how Stormy would feel about staying in it.

"We should really do something about this room," Alexander said to Jameson. "Don't you think?"

"Yes, it needs a feminine touch," Jameson said. Both Romanians looked to me.

"Really?" I asked, excited for a chance to decorate more of the Mansion. "I'd love to!

"So . . . what does she like?" I imagined all the things we'd need as I sized up the room. "We could buy rugs, curtains, and maybe a cool chair?"

"She's just visiting, not moving in," Alexander said.

"Oh yeah . . ." I said, realizing I was getting ahead of myself.

"But no—you're right," he added. "I don't want her running back to my parents saying she didn't like it here."

"So what are her favorite things?" I asked.

"I don't know." Then my boyfriend thought for a moment. He noticed my Hello Batty earrings. "She loves Hello Batty."

"Oh, cool!"

"You have something in common already," he said, tenderly patting my arm.

"We also have you," I said, flashing him a warm smile.

Alexander returned mine with a radiant grin.

"Does she like Olivia Outcast, too?" I wondered out loud.

"I think so."

"What's her favorite color?" I asked Alexander. "Black? Pink? Red?" I didn't really know anything about Stormy except that she was Alexander's sister. And just because she was a vampire didn't mean she liked dark things. Maybe she was blonde with little tiny fairy-tale locks. Then I thought of Luna—did she look like her? I couldn't bear the thought.

"Uh . . . I know she loves purple."

"Of course! We can put some girlie things in her room, like purple curtains and a funky velvet chair. She would love that! I can picture her already. I'll put out some candy on the table and a gift bag on her dresser."

"Sure," Alexander said. "I didn't even think of that before now, but I'm sure she'd feel much better in something cute and fun rather than this cold, barren room."

"I can't wait to meet her," I said enthusiastically. "I've never had a little sister."

For a moment I dreamed about the perfect sister for me—a younger sibling who would want to have picnics in the cemeteries, stay up late and watch scary-movie marathons, and share dark music together. She'd be nothing like the sibling I had, Billy, a little brother who would rather solve math equations than hang around tombstones.

"Well, I've never had a younger brother," Alexander said. "That would be really cool, too."

"Can we trade?" I asked seriously.

"Sure," he said, but I could tell by the glint in his eyes he wasn't as keen on giving his sibling away as I was.

It was hard to find anything fun and funky in Dullsville that would be appropriate or cool for Stormy. I bought most of my clothes and trinkets at thrift stores or online.

Becky and I shopped at our local discount superstore while Jameson waited for us at the front by the coffee shop.

I got my usual stares as we paraded up and down the aisles looking for anything fun to decorate Stormy's room.

"This is nice of you, to try so hard to make Alexander's sister comfortable," Becky said as I tossed a purple fleece pillow into our cart.

"How can I not make the effort? I think it will be cool to have her here, even if it is only for a short while."

"I don't know." Becky handed me a neon-green lamp. I shook my head, and she put it back on the shelf. "I don't have a little sister. This is foreign territory to me. But whatever we do will be fine. You're Alexander's girlfriend. She'll love you, too."

"Aww, thanks." I suddenly felt the pressure relieved.

"What do you do to decorate a room for a vampire?" she asked aloud.

Two elderly women glared at us, bewildered.

"Shh!" I said under my breath.

"Oops," Becky said, startled by the ladies overhearing her. "For Halloween," Becky corrected loudly. "We're shopping for Halloween."

We quickly pushed our carts around the gawking ladies and headed for the next aisle, where we burst out laughing.

"That was close," she said. "I don't know how you do it."

"Welcome to my world," I remarked.

"All this secrecy," she whispered. "It's very difficult."

"But it makes it all that much more exciting, right?"

Becky shrugged her shoulders. She was still getting used to the revelation that the Underworld existed and that it was as close as my boyfriend.

"What about this?" I asked, pointing at velvety lavender

curtains that were displayed with other sample curtains.

"Ooh. Cool. Maybe you can decorate my room next?"

"Sure!" I answered, delighted.

"Only you'll have to stay away from blood-reds."

"If you insist."

Becky peered out the end of the aisle and into the main part of the store. I followed her. "Are there any vampires here?" she whispered.

"No, just one wannabe."

"How do you know?" she asked with a hush. "How do you know that everyone here isn't a vampire?"

We glanced around. A sample of Dullsville's population permeated the store: couples, families, teens.

"I don't think there has ever been a vampire in this store," I answered with a laugh.

"What about Jameson?" she asked, looking toward where he was waiting for us near the checkout. "Is he a vampire?"

"I don't know. . . . He goes out during the day," I said.

"Maybe he's part vampire and part mortal." Becky said. "He sure looks that way."

Becky's comment left me feeling curious about Alexander's butler.

"Well, I don't think we've left anything for any other visiting vampires," she said, assessing our selections.

Our carts were full of fun stuff that I thought Stormy might like: pillows, candles, wall hangings, a few scatter rugs and assembly-required furniture to make her space more comfortable.

"I think we're all set," I said, and we headed over to the Creepy Man and his credit card.

Alexander hung up the curtains, and Becky and I placed the scatter rugs on the floor in Stormy's new room. There was so much dust there, Becky went into a coughing fit.

My boyfriend was attractive even in the dim lighting as he worked as hard as a handsome handyman.

"Is this straight?" he asked. I'd never realized Alexander was such a perfectionist. The drapes hung flawlessly.

Now that the curtains were hung and the funky furniture and shelves were installed, we placed a few ornaments on the antique dresser. Alexander had painted tiny pictures of his family, and I fitted them into frames we'd purchased.

"She'll love this," Alexander said, examining the room.

"Do you think so?" I asked. I thought the room was fabulous, but since I hadn't met Stormy yet, it was hard to know if she would. I could only count on Alexander for his opinion.

"Hey, what's not to like?" Alexander said, sizing up our room makeover. "This place is awesome!"

"I think so, too," Becky concurred. "I love how you transformed this room."

"I'm glad you both think so," I said, wiping my hair away from my face. "But this is really your grandmother's home. Stormy might be offended that I decorated it."

"Well, now it's my home, too. And besides, my grandmother would be happy to know that you are going to so much trouble for my sister."

"I had a great time doing this," I said. "I'm glad you think your grandmother would approve."

"Well, more importantly, Stormy will. She is very opinionated. And this is way cooler than her room at home," Alexander added.

"I agree, Raven, you've outdone yourself," Becky said. "She's going to love it here!"

"Did Stormy ever visit the Mansion when you were growing up?" I asked Alexander.

"Just as a baby. I don't think she remembers it. She was so little." Alexander beamed as he gazed at our accomplishment and put his arm around my shoulder. "The only problem is now she'll never want to leave!"

A few days later, Stormy was set to arrive in Dullsville. I was so excited to meet her, I skipped dinner and waited for the sun to set outside the Mansion. I remembered how anxious I had been to meet Alexander's parents. I'd imagined what they were like and worried what kind of impression I'd make. This time, I wasn't as nervous, but I was hoping Alexander's sister and I would get along smoothly. When the door finally opened, I greeted Alexander with a huge kiss. I was pacing around the Mansion, the yummy smell of Jameson's dinner in the warmer wafting throughout, while Alexander lay on the antique sofa, flipping through a modern art magazine as we waited for Jameson's Mercedes to pull in.

"I think I hear a car," I said, running to the door.

"That's the tenth time you've said that," he said, not looking up from the mag.

"I'm sure it's them this time," I said, happily twisting the doorknob.

"That's not the Mercedes," Alexander called as I opened the door, as if he knew with his vampire sixth sense.

Disappointed, I thought it best to wait it out with Alexander. And why not? We had so little alone-time anymore that I might as well take advantage of it. I snuggled up to him on the sofa and was leaning my head on his chest when I heard a car on the street. The sound got louder with each passing moment, and bright lights shined on the Mansion. I knew this had to be Jameson's ride. We both sat up.

I poked my head against the window and peered out into the night.

I saw two headlights and a black car illuminated from the streetlight. "It's them! It's Jameson's car."

Alexander couldn't hide his enthusiasm from me as he, too, beamed. We headed to the door, and after he opened it I followed him outside to the parked car. Jameson said good evening to us as he slowly came around the back of the car.

I did my best to catch a glimpse of Stormy, but all I could see was dark hair.

I waited with bated breath to see Alexander's little sister.

Jameson politely opened her door and out stepped Stormy Sterling.

Stormy was rail thin and stood about five feet two. She had straight bangs and shoulder-length jet-black hair. Her nails were bitten and chipped; charcoal-colored nail polish remained. Midnight-colored lipstick stained her small lips. She had rubber bracelets and a black-and-white headband. Tiny silver studs and hoops ran up the sides of her tiny ear-lobes. Her shirt was lacy, and her tights were ripped in all the trendy and cool places. She wore mini-monster boots and black fingerless lace gloves.

She was everything I dreamed she'd be.

"Alexander!" she called in a sweet voice.

Stormy raced over to him, and he enveloped her in his arms.

"It's great to see you!" she squealed.

"It's great to see you, too!" It was obvious how much he had missed his sister as he continued to hug her.

They eventually let go. Stormy giggled. "We have full reign without parents! We are going to have the time of our lives!"

I hung back until she noticed me.

Alexander swooped in with gentlemanly introductions. "This is Raven. Raven, this is my sister, Athena," he said. "But her friends call her Stormy."

"It is a pleasure to meet you." She extended her hand. Stormy was precious.

"I'm so excited you're here!" I gushed, just like I hoped I wouldn't.

I wanted to run up and hug Stormy—the sister I'd always wanted. Only I knew when I was her age—and even now—how awkward it was when an older person acted all gooey on me when we had barely even been intro-duced. It always felt fake, though in this case it would have been genuine. Instead of squeezing her to bits, I kept my distance.

She smiled a polite smile, exposing white plastic braces adorned with purple and black rubber bands, with small vampire fangs peeking out below them.

But then her smile soured. "Oh no! I forgot Phantom!"

We turned to the car, and Jameson held in his stick-pin arms a ghost-white cat with pink eyes.

"Jameson! Thank you!" Stormy rushed over and held her cat.

"You are quite welcome, Miss Athena."

"She's cute," I whispered to Alexander. "Just like you."

"You'll love it here, Phantom," she cooed to her cat. "Just like I will."

Alexander noticed Jameson grabbing Stormy's suitcase and backpack from the trunk.

"I can get that, Jameson," Alexander offered.

"Thank you, but no need," the Creepy Man said. "You greet your sister."

"Let's go inside," Alexander said. "I'm sure you're hungry."

"Awesome! I can't wait for a smoothie with cherries and a purple sword!" Stormy exclaimed.

"Of course, Miss Athena," the Creepy Man said with a toothy smile.

Stormy raced into the Mansion. "Here I am!" she declared to the empty foyer.

Alexander beamed again.

"This is so awesome," she continued to Alexander.

"I'm going to have so much fun here with you!"

He tousled her hair like only a big brother could.

"I do remember—it's all the same," she said, smoothing out her hair. "This isn't fair!" she exclaimed. "You get full reign of this place without Mother and Father looking over your shoulder."

Jameson placed her bags by the staircase. "Dinner won't be long. Then I'll unpack your things, Miss Athena, as you settle in." He creeped slowly toward the kitchen.

"Which room is mine?" she asked.

"You'll have to guess," Alexander said. "But I think you'll know it when you see it. Raven helped me decorate."

"She did?" Her eyes squinted, and her voice couldn't hide her skepticism. I knew there was a chance she'd resent me decorating parts of the Mansion, and here it was before me. She pushed a smile out as hard as she could. "That was very kind of you," she said, overly polite.

Alexander put his arm around her bony shoulder as the two walked up the staircase. I knew it was important to let the two siblings have their time together.

"I can help Jameson," I said from the bottom of the staircase.

"You have to come up, too," Alexander directed.

I was anxious when we reached the top of the stairs. My heart thrummed the way it might if I was throwing a surprise party and hoping that the recipient was indeed surprised.

By the looks of Stormy's style, I thought maybe she'd like how I decorated her room, but there was a huge chance

57

I could have missed the mark on her taste and she'd see the room as a big disaster. I held my breath as Alexander lit several candles, illuminating her room. Though the vampires could see in the dark, the soft light helped us all see the room's interior even better.

She paused and glanced around.

"This . . . is . . ."

"Yes?" Alexander asked, waiting for her reaction.

"Gorgeous! It's just fabulous!" she exclaimed.

Even Phantom examined her new surroundings by jumping on the chaise longue and sniffing at the stuffed animals.

I breathed a sigh of relief, and it appeared that Alexander had been anxious, too, as his sigh was audible.

She raced over to the chaise longue, hopped on it, and hugged a few of the pillows.

"And this Hello Batty plush!" she said, holding it up. "Do I get to keep it?"

"Everything is yours," Alexander said.

"We can put your coffin right here," Alexander said, pointing to the only empty area.

His words sent goose bumps over my flesh. A coffin. For a girl to sleep in. It was so awesome!

Stormy buzzed around the room, touching everything she saw. "I love these candles!" she said, sniffing the lavender scent. "And these picture frames—with your paintings of us, Alexander! These look exactly like Mother and Father. And these curtains! They are so long and luscious!" She draped them over herself as if they were a ball gown. "How do I look?"

"Like a movie star!" Alexander said.

"I can't believe you did all this for me."

"Well, actually," he said, "Raven did. You know that I don't have a clue about buying frilly pillows," Alexander said.

"But I thought you did it with her," she began.

"Well, Alexander put everything together," I said.

"Not really. Raven picked out everything and designed it."

"You did?" she asked. "How did you know what I liked?"

"Alexander told me."

"But Raven found everything," Alexander said proudly. "She did a great job, didn't she?"

"Yes." She nodded enthusiastically. Then she asked, "Did Luna help?"

Luna? There was that name.

"No," Alexander said. "Why would Luna help? This was all Raven. You have her to thank for your room."

Alexander genuinely meant that the work I'd done was a sincere gesture from me to Stormy, but I was afraid she'd be upset that someone other than her own family—a stranger to her— had decorated her room. I couldn't blame her if those were her true feelings.

"Thank you so much, Raven. I love it!" she said, twisting her jet-black locks. It was as if she thought about hugging me but didn't know what to do. Instead, she flashed me a smile and hopped again on the chaise longue with Phantom.

"You don't have to thank me," I said. "I had a great time doing it."

Jameson came into the room and placed Stormy's luggage by the dresser. "I'll bring her coffin up, too."

The Creepy Man was frail, and I couldn't imagine him bringing a casket up the Mansion staircase or even assembling one on his own. Fortunately, neither could Alexander.

"No," Alexander said. "I'll get that."

"Thank you. Dinner will be ready in a few moments," the butler said.

Stormy hopped off the chaise longue and straightened her skirt. Jameson left, and Alexander and I watched as Stormy surveyed all the trinkets I'd placed on her bookshelf.

She grinned slightly, and I could tell by her expression that she was really pleased with her new digs.

"So where is Raven's room?" she asked suddenly.

Alexander was taken aback by her direct question and chuckled nervously. "At her house," Alexander replied.

"You don't live here, too?" she asked me as if she was expecting I did.

"No," I said. "I live with my family. And they are not as exciting as yours. Believe me."

Stormy seemed slightly relieved knowing I hadn't taken physical custody of the Mansion and she had power over her rightful territory.

"You must be hungry," Alexander said. "Let's hit the kitchen."

Alexander blew out the candles, and we followed

Stormy out of her room until she paused at the top of the stairs and turned to look at us.

"Are you two getting married?" she suddenly blurted out like a typical younger sibling.

I laughed, and Alexander cracked a crooked smile.

Stormy and I waited to hear Alexander's response. I wasn't sure how she wanted him to respond, but I knew how I did.

Alexander put his hand on his sister's shoulder and guided her down the staircase. "Jameson!" he called. "We're coming down to dinner!"

I think we were both disappointed not to get an answer.

We sat down to eat in the formal dining room, which was dressed with gleaming silver, fine china, and linen napkins. Several candelabras lit the room, and the red candle wax dripped like a bleeding wound. Alexander pulled out Stormy's chair, seating her to the left of him, and I followed suit at his right. Stormy and I faced each other across the table, with Alexander in the middle at the head of the table. Stormy, so cool and stylish in her lacy black fingerless gloves, placed her linen napkin gingerly on her lap.

Jameson pushed the dining cart in from the kitchen and served us a nice dinner of rare filets (medium well for me), twice-baked potatoes, and peas. Stormy had a blood-filled glass goblet garnished with a cherry and a purple sword, while Alexander also had a blood-filled goblet. Mine was filled with boring old soda.

When Stormy lowered her goblet after her first sip, red liquid dotted the corners of her lips. Alexander gestured to her, and she rolled her eyes at him. When she wiped it off, the dark liquid smeared the light napkin. I was shocked. I'd seen wine-stained napkins before, but this was the first time I'd seen a bloodstained one.

"So, what have you been up to?" Alexander asked as he cut his juicy steak.

"Nothing much," she said. "Home isn't the same without you there." Stormy cut her steak into tiny little pieces. She savored each bite.

"Oh, come on," Alexander challenged. "You are always busy with something."

She rolled her chocolate-brown eyes. "Well, you've been gone a long time. How can I tell you everything?"

"What do you mean?" Alexander took a bite of his meal.

"You were only supposed to be gone until the Maxwell feud was over," she said, pushing her peas around with her fork. "And it is. Once you took Valentine back to Jagger, it was over. But you didn't come home. You stayed here." She didn't look at me. She didn't have to. I could feel the tension from the younger Sterling as if she blamed me for his absence.

"I know," he said. "But I have a life here now, too. So what is so different without me?"

"The house is so big. I have no one to talk to."

"We didn't talk all the time," he said.

"I know. But it was nice having you there. That's where you live, remember?"

"Well, I live here. For now. Mom and Dad told you that."

"I know. But it's so far away. You get to have all the fun. It's not fair."

"I'm sure you have fun, too."

"I do not. Not like you. You get to meet a lot of people. You get to do what you want."

"I'm eighteen," he said. "When I was twelve, I didn't get to do everything that I wanted. Besides, I could be going to college soon, anyway. You have to get used to my being away."

"But this is different," she said.

"Why?"

"You know why. . . ." she hinted.

"Maybe we should talk about this later? You just got here."

I thought it best to divert the conversation. "Are you homeschooled like Alexander?" I asked Stormy.

"Yes."

"Do you like that?" I wondered.

"I guess so," she said. I was surprised she wasn't more excited.

"I'm jealous of that. I think it would be so cool. Hanging out at home. Getting to watch TV."

"I don't get to watch TV."

"You don't?"

"It's like jail."

"It is not," Alexander said with a laugh.

"Not to you," she said. "You are here."

"I call this town Dullsville," I said, "and I say that for a reason."

"C'mon. You have a great time," Alexander said. "You study, you travel. You have a lot of friends."

"I do not!" she said. "I don't even have a boyfriend."

"Well, you have plenty of time for that." Alexander was emphatic.

"I'm twelve! I get just as thirsty as you do."

Alexander cleared his throat.

"I can't believe you don't have friends," I said. "I bet you have tons."

"Yes, a few. But I don't have a boyfriend, and the only guy I get to hang out with is Valentine."

"Valentine Maxwell?" I asked, referring to the Maxwell twins' younger sibling. He was my brother Billy's age. Billy, his friend Henry, and Valentine had hung out together when Valentine came to Dullsville in search of his older siblings. Instead he found a friendly clique with Billy and Henry and tried to become blood brothers with them. But soon Valentine grew thirsty, and without another to feed on or a bottled-blood-filled cellar like the Mansion's, Valentine grew weak. Alexander returned Valentine to a thankful Jagger in Hipsterville, and the feud with the Maxwells was over.

"Ooh, do you like him?" I pried.

"He's cute."

"He is?" Alexander asked, surprised. "I've never heard you talk about him that way."

"But I want to meet new guys. And Mother and Father keep me studying too much of the time."

"Well, your education is very important," Alexander said.

"Ugh," she said. "You would say that. You all want me locked up forever."

"You are not locked up," he said. "Quit being so dramatic."

"I am; you don't even know. You don't mind painting in your room for hours. But I want to be out and seeing the world."

"Well, you are here, now," he said. "This is getting out into the world."

She made a face at her brother. "I know. I'm glad I'm here."

"So what do you like to do for fun?" I asked.

"Uh . . . I read and write poems."

"And try to sneak out of the house?" Alexander teased.

"Just sometimes," she said with an impish smile.

"I do that, too," I said.

"You do?" She gazed at me skeptically.

"Well, I really sneak in more places than I sneak out of. In fact, that's the first time I saw Alexander face-to-face. Right there—" I said, pointing to the bottom of the staircase.

Alexander cleared his throat again.

"It's no secret," I said.

"Secret?" she asked eagerly. "Tell me!"

I leaned forward. "I snuck into the Mansion."

"You did?" Again she was skeptical.

"Yes," I answered proudly. "And it wasn't the first time."

"Maybe she shouldn't hear all this," Alexander said.

"No, tell me." Stormy was keen to hear more. "I must know."

"I used to sneak in here when I was younger."

"Why would you want to sneak *in*?" she wondered.

"I wanted to see what was on the inside."

"Funny, I've always wanted to see what is on the outside," she said.

"Well, we will get to that tomorrow," Alexander said as we finished our desserts.

It wasn't long before Alexander was preparing to take me home. I was grabbing my coat in the foyer when I overheard the two siblings talking in the kitchen. I knew I should let the two of them talk privately, but I couldn't help myself. It wasn't like me *not* to eavesdrop.

I tiptoed over to the kitchen's entryway and hung outside of view.

"So what are we going to do here?" I heard Stormy ask. "I want to see the town. And Luna."

"We'll see her sometime."

"But when? I've missed her so much."

"I don't know."

"I can't wait to see her."

"But don't you think Raven's cool?"

"Yes, she is very pretty. Mother and Father raved about her when they came home."

"They did?" His voice was bright.

"All they talked about for a week straight was Raven." Her voice grew dark.

"Well, I know you guys will be fast friends."

There was a pause.

"Why haven't you come home?" Stormy asked softly. "Is it because of me?"

"You know I had to leave. For the family. There was too much turmoil if I stayed. Why would it be because of you?"

"I wasn't sure if you were mad at me—from the night of the covenant ceremony."

"I couldn't be mad at you. It was my decision."

"But I was so angry."

"I understood. Everyone was upset."

"But it's been a year. You weren't supposed to stay this long."

"I like it here," he said.

"And you like Raven."

"Yes, I do."

"But why . . . why didn't you turn Luna? She's beautiful and so much fun! All you had to do was turn her. Then we all could be together in Romania. And she could have been a vampire—a *Sterling* vampire."

"She wasn't the right girl for me. I'm sorry to have disappointed you. But Luna is doing fine. She doesn't need me to get along in this world."

"Well, now that Luna is a vampire, why don't you like her?" she asked.

"Stormy . . . I wasn't . . . it just wasn't right. You'll understand when you're older."

"I understand now. You don't think I know about love?"

"If you do . . . well, you'll know that you need to wait for the one you really love."

"So you didn't love Luna?"

I didn't hear him answer. I figured he was shaking his head.

"You love Raven?"

He was quiet again. I was hoping he was nodding this time.

"We don't have to talk about all this tonight," Alexander finally said, "do we?"

Just then I stepped back into the room.

Stormy looked at me as if she wondered how much I'd heard.

"We were just catching up a bit," Alexander said. "I kind of left home in a hurry. Not the best situation. But now we're together—"

"Yes," she said. Stormy flashed a grin.

"I'm going to take Raven home," he said to his sibling. "Maybe you can take a catnap?"

"But it's only midnight," she whined.

"I know—but you've traveled quite a bit."

"I'm not a child," she said, just as I probably would have in her situation.

It was odd to leave and have to be the one going to bed while a twelve-year-old girl got to stay awake until sunrise. Being a mortal had its drawbacks. "It was nice to finally meet you, Stormy," I said. "I hope to see you again soon."

"Yes, it was lovely meeting you, Raven," she said with a sweet grin. I was hoping for a hug, but it didn't happen. She politely offered her hand instead.

I gently shook it, and she raced up the grand staircase, just like I had a hundred times before.

I felt kind of lonely, knowing that I had to go home while the siblings got to hang out together. But this was really about Alexander and not me, and I took comfort in knowing that his loneliness, living in the Mansion with just Jameson for company, was minimized again.

"She seems really sweet," I said when Alexander and I had settled into the Mercedes.

"I'm glad you like her," he said.

"What's not to like?" I asked.

He shrugged his shoulders.

"Why do you call her Stormy?" I asked when we drove down the long and winding drive.

"She has her moments."

"Really? She seems very polite."

"She is. But she can be very vocal and dramatic."

"Like me?"

"Yes, I'd say that," he said with a chuckle.

Then I remembered the private chat that I'd overheard. "I don't want her to resent me," I said.

"Why would she? She just likes to be the center of attention, that's all. She always has."

"No, I mean that you didn't return to Romania. She might think that you are still here because of me."

"Well, I am." Alexander sported a reassuring smile.

"But it's your decision," I said. "She needs to know that. Otherwise she'll just blame me."

"You think so?"

"I know so. I just wanted you to know, too."

Alexander paused for a moment, as if he was giving my words real thought.

"Maybe sometime this week you two can spend some girl-time together," he said. "Then she'll know exactly why I fell in love with you, too."

I waited impatiently in my family room in anticipation of Alexander picking me up. He was taking Stormy to visit the Crypt, and he wanted the three of us to go together. I knew Luna would be at the club and that Stormy was looking forward to seeing her. I had hoped for a little more time for Stormy and me to bond before she reunited with Luna, but I was excited that I was going to be with Alexander to show her the club. When the doorbell rang, I raced to the door. I got a few heavenly smooches in before Alexander led me to the Mercedes. When we reached the car, Stormy was sitting in the front seat. Alexander shot her a look and gestured for her to hop in the back. Billy Boy and I had spent many travels fighting for the front seat of the car. I knew how important it was for a younger sibling to sit in the front, so I opened the back door.

"No," Alexander said. "Stormy will sit in the back."

I heard a large "humph!" from her. I was okay with riding in the backseat. After all, she wasn't Billy Boy, and it really had been more about our sibling power struggle than about looking out the front window.

Stormy started to open her door, but I jumped into the backseat.

"It's okay," I said. "I like it back here. I feel like I'm being chauffeured."

Stormy shrugged her shoulders as Alexander sneered at her.

"All right," he said, changing his mood. "Off to the Crypt."

"I can't wait to see it," Stormy said. "I've never been to a club before. So will there be boys my age there?" she asked.

"Uh . . . not usually," Alexander said.

"Who am I going to dance with?" she asked.

"We'll all dance together," I offered.

"Oh . . ." She was audibly disappointed, and her voice trailed off as she gazed out the window.

Alexander turned into the gravel lot, and Stormy was amazed by the size of the factory. "This is the club?" she asked.

"Part of it is," Alexander said.

"What's in the other parts?" she said, wondering.

"Jagger's office," Alexander said, parking. "Their sleeping quarters. A covenant altar."

"They have a covenant altar in this place?"

"Yes," Alexander said. "Jagger doesn't leave anything out."

"Wow—this is so fabulous!" she exclaimed, hopping from the car.

"I thought you might like it," he said as we got out and joined her. "You could be the youngest one there."

"So Luna and Jagger sleep here?" she asked as she looked up at the huge abandoned factory. Large windows were missing and, from the alley, one could see discarded boxes filling some of the rooms.

"Yes," Alexander replied.

"The Maxwells don't have an apartment?" she asked.

"I think they feel this is their apartment."

"I want to sleep here, too!"

We waited at the end of a small line that had formed. When we reached the entrance, the burly security guard looked us over and took a moment when he saw Stormy.

"Is this your sister?" he asked me.

"No. She's *his* sister."

"I would have sworn you two were sisters," he said, gesturing to Stormy and me. "The same hair, the same style."

I was flattered, but I wasn't sure if Stormy felt the same. I glanced over to catch her expression, and she had a huge grin on her face. I was hoping she wasn't just being polite.

We stepped into the club, and Stormy was entranced by her new environment.

"This is stellar!"

Among the crowd of clubsters, it was obvious that Stormy was the youngest one in attendance. I was proud to be in the company of Alexander and his sister. It felt so amazing to be walking into a fabulously morbid dance club in Dullsville in the company of my vampire boyfriend and his younger vampire sibling. It wasn't something I'd ever imagined happening—and here I was doing it.

"Look at all the tombstones," she said, pointing to the walls. "I feel so at home."

That was exactly how I felt. It was like I was standing next to a younger version of myself.

"Where's Luna?" Stormy asked. "I want to see her."

"We have plenty of time to run into her," Alexander answered. "Raven and I will show you around."

"Yes, look over here," I said to Stormy. I led her to the coffins Jagger had in the corner of the club. Several club-sters were lying inside and mugging for their friends.

"Aren't these awesome?" I asked enthusiastically.

As soon as I said that, I realized how mundane these were to her. For the mortals in Dullsville, this was freaky and fun. But Stormy always slept in a coffin. It was like someone being excited to show me beds at a mattress factory. And on top of that, she couldn't even be photographed. I'd missed the mark on two vampire points.

"Uh . . . cute," she said politely.

I rolled my eyes at myself and led her back to Alexander.

"Did you find Luna?" she asked.

"No," Alexander answered. "She's not that fond of me, you know."

I was surprised how clueless Alexander was about Luna. And I was surprised she wasn't draping herself all over him the moment I left him unattended. I thought she might be hanging out by the bar with Romeo, so I guided us away from that area to give us more of a chance to be together.

Just then I spotted Scarlet and Becky talking at the edge of the dance floor.

"Where are your better halves?" I asked.

"Practice," Scarlet said, obviously bummed.

"Aren't they always practicing?" I whined.

"Yes," Becky replied. "That's why they are so good."

"Is this Stormy?" Scarlet asked.

"Yes, how did you know?" I wondered.

"Luna mentioned she was coming tonight. I'm Scarlet," she said, turning to the younger Sterling.

"Pleased to meet you," Stormy said, extending her hand, which Scarlet shook.

"Wow, she's so cute and polite," Scarlet said.

Alexander beamed proudly.

"And I'm Becky," Becky said, extending her hand to Alexander's sister.

"Becky has been my best friend since third grade," I said to Stormy as the two shook hands.

Stormy eyed us both as if she didn't believe me. I guessed it might seem weird to a stranger, since Becky and I were polar opposites in appearance.

"Why don't we all dance?" Scarlet asked.

Just then Sebastian found us. "Hey, girl!" he said, and swooped Stormy up in his arms. Even though she clearly wanted to be treated like an adult, Sebastian grabbed her like she was a child, and she shrieked in his embrace as if she was one.

"How are you?" he asked, setting her down.

"I'm fabulous," she said.

"Still have those braces?" he teased.

"Yes, but I'll be getting them off soon."

"I think I like them on you. Those purple and black bands are sexy!"

Stormy giggled with delight.

Jagger spotted us from the bar and gave a polite wave to Stormy.

Stormy didn't know how to respond. She hung next to Alexander and Sebastian as he headed over to us.

"It's okay," Alexander said. "Remember, our feud is over."

"I don't trust him," she said with a whisper. "I never have."

"So we have a guest here?" Jagger said, his green and blue eyes shining down at her.

"Yes, Stormy came to visit me," Alexander said.

"And one of her first stops was this club?" Jagger asked, pleased.

Alexander reluctantly nodded his head.

"She came to dance with me," Sebastian said.

Jagger shot him a glare but turned his attention back to

Stormy. "Well then, you've come to the right place. What do you think of it?"

"I love it!" she said genuinely.

Jagger beamed with pride. "I thought this town needed something like this to give it some life."

"Well, it sure has," I chimed in. "You are doing so well here."

"I'm glad you think so," he said. "And I'm hoping the club will get even better." He eyed me with a lingering stare. It made me slightly anxious; I wasn't sure what he meant by the comment.

"Is Luna here?" Stormy asked Jagger.

"Yes, she's buzzing about here somewhere. I know she was looking forward to seeing you."

"I can't wait to see her," Stormy said eagerly.

"I saw her a few minutes ago. I think she was talking to Romeo. They are quite the item, you know," he said specifically to Sebastian.

Sebastian glared at Jagger, who slipped into the crowd. Then Sebastian turned to Stormy. "So am I going to get that dance?" he asked, offering his hand.

She nodded enthusiastically.

"Hey—" Scarlet said. "We asked her first."

"Fine, why don't we all dance?" Sebastian winked at Onyx, who couldn't help but smile.

"That sounds like fun," Stormy said. Just as they started for the dance floor, I saw pink hair bobbing our way. Within a few moments, she broke through the crowd and there stood Luna in all her glory.

"Stormy Girl!" Luna called, her twiggy arms outstretched.

"Luna!" Stormy ran to her like I'd wished she'd run to me when I first met her. Luna picked up the young Sterling and swung her around. They giggled and squealed exuberantly. Their embrace was that of best friends reuniting after years of separation.

Luna fiddled with Stormy's hair and bracelets as the two girls talked.

I tried not to sulk openly, but Alexander must have sensed my awkward feelings.

"It's okay," he said, patting me on the shoulder. "They've known each other for years."

"I know. . . ." I said. Normally I didn't care what people thought of me, but Stormy was different. I really hoped for a friendly relationship with Alexander's sister.

Luna took Stormy by the wrist and led her out onto the dance floor, leaving Scarlet, Becky, and me on the sidelines.

"Pure evil," Scarlet mumbled.

"Yes," Becky said. "Luna acted as if we weren't even here."

"I ought to pummel her," Scarlet snarled.

"It's okay," I said. I didn't want to start trouble, and I really wanted Stormy to have fun while she was in town. And if that meant being with Luna rather than being with us, I had to be the bigger person and accept that.

Stormy and Luna bopped up and down like firecrackers. Alexander's sister was having a great time. And though I'd wished she was having it with me, I was pleased that she was enjoying her visit, regardless.

"How's it going so far?" Becky asked.

"I think really well."

"I knew you'd hit it off," she said supportively.

I pulled Becky aside while Scarlet went to find Onyx. "But there's this whole Luna thing."

"Yes, I see."

"It's like Luna is trying to take her away—to show me that she is a better friend to her than I can ever be. Like she wants to throw it in my face that she and Alexander's little sister are BFFs or something."

"That's Luna," Becky said resignedly. "She's always sticking it to you."

"I know. But this time she's right."

"So, Luna knew her first. What's the big deal?"

"I think Stormy wanted Alexander to . . ." I began but then stopped. I realized I hadn't told Becky the real story about Alexander and Luna's history. "Uh . . . never mind."

"No, tell me. Is it about them being vampires?"

"Yes."

"Then I have to know! Tell me."

"Okay . . . The Maxwells and the Sterlings had an agreement that Luna and Alexander would have a covenant ceremony. Kind of like an arranged marriage, only a covenant ceremony bonds two together for eternity."

"Wow—that's a long time."

"Yes, and Luna wasn't even a vampire then. So when he'd bite her she'd turn into a vampire and they'd be together forever."

"Like you want?"

"Yes."

"So, did he do it?"

"No. Thank goodness."

Becky smiled.

"Alexander didn't love her. And he didn't want to turn someone he didn't love."

"Aww, he was waiting for you," Becky said.

"But he hadn't met me yet."

"But he was *waiting* to meet you."

"You think I'm the one?" I asked.

"Yes. Of course," Becky said, smiling.

I loved being reassured that Alexander might think of me in that way, even though he had told me so himself. But since he hadn't turned me yet, I liked knowing that it could possibly happen in the future.

But I still wondered if Alexander were to turn me, when would it be? How long would I have to wait? I wondered if I'd be an old lady and he'd still be youthful looking. Did Alexander even think about a time for us to take that plunge together?

"So tell me more," Becky said, breaking me out of my trance. "I'm dying to know all the juicy details!"

"Oh yeah. There was a big feud between the families when Alexander refused to have the covenant ceremony with Luna, and that's when Alexander left Romania to come here to Dullsville to live in his grandmother's mansion."

"Wow—that sounds really hard. Having to leave your family and come to a foreign country and live alone." Her voice was filled with concern, as if she was imagining that as her own fate. "And all of that, just to get away from Luna and Jagger?"

"Yes. Only the Maxwells followed him. Jagger was seeking revenge for his family's humiliation."

Becky's eyes grew wide. "Wow. That's why they came here?"

"Yes."

She paused, really thinking the change of events through. "Wait, you said Alexander didn't turn Luna. But isn't she a vampire now? How did that happen?"

"Yes, someone else turned her. But she still wants to be bonded with someone—Alexander, really—and that's why she tried with Sebastian. So she could be close to Alexander. But now I'm hoping she'll fall in love with Romeo."

"I didn't know any of this. I wish you'd have told me sooner."

"I just couldn't. Not until you knew about Alexander. About him being a . . ."

"Yes, I understand. Don't worry—but what about Luna now?"

"I don't think she got over it—or him. And how can I blame her?"

"It is hard. You feel compassion for her—but yet you want Alexander for yourself."

"And now I'm learning that Stormy felt spurned, too. She wanted Alexander to fall in love with her babysitter, Luna. Only he didn't."

"He fell in love with you."

I patted my friend's arm as a thank-you.

"But don't feel guilty," she told me. "You are way cooler than Luna."

"Aww, thanks," I said. "But I don't think Stormy sees it that way."

"Well, she will."

I glanced over at the pink- and black-haired girls dancing as if no one else was in the club. They seemed to be having so much fun, I wasn't sure how I'd be able to fit into the mix.

"Alexander said we'd spend some girl-time together," I went on. "Just Stormy and me. I'm looking forward to getting to know her one-on-one."

"Well, just relax," she said. "Alexander is the one you really want to like you. And by the looks of it, I know he feels he's made the right decision."

I turned and caught Alexander staring at me. He must have been watching me while I talked to Becky. I ran over to him and squeezed him with all my might. If he hadn't followed his heart that night in Romania, I'd never have mine filled with love the way I did today.

Alexander handed me a soda, and eventually Stormy joined us. She was hot and sticky, her bangs stuck to her forehead, her charcoal eyeliner bleeding.

Alexander flagged Romeo, and he handed Alexander a drink. The liquid was red, so I assumed it was blood. Alexander gave the drink to his sister and she quickly gulped in down.

"Can I sleep here after sunrise?" she asked. "Luna asked me to."

"Yes, she can sleep with us," Luna said excitedly. She stood behind Stormy and wrapped her lithe arms around her shoulders. "It'll be a blast."

I turned to Alexander.

"Please?" Stormy whined.

"But you just got here," Alexander said. "You don't want to hang out with me?"

"Of course I do. But I haven't seen Luna in forever. It's just one sleepover."

"Well . . ." Alexander began, thinking.

"I'll take good care of her," Luna insisted.

"She babysat me for a million years," Stormy said. "It'll only be this one time."

Alexander looked to me for an answer. I wasn't going to be the one to say no.

"Please, Alexander?" Stormy asked.

"Well . . . all right," he said.

All right? I thought. Just like that? Becky and I would have felt we needed to observe the girl the whole time. But Alexander was a guy and since he knew she'd be okay, he just wanted her to be happy.

"I will pick you up tomorrow just after sunset," he said. "Not a minute later."

"Thank you!" She gave Alexander a hug and me a friendly wave. Luna shot me a devilish smile and a glance that meant she had won.

I sidled up close to Luna. "Stormy might know you longer than she knows me, but I'm the one going home with Alexander," I whispered to the Maxwell twin, and headed for the exit. When Alexander and I were outside the club, I stopped and turned to him. "Why did you let her stay?"

"This will give us a chance to have some time together," he said. He pulled me in to him, and his deep, dark eyes stared into mine. "I haven't been able to kiss you properly in nights."

Then he leaned in and kissed me with such tenderness and passion that I forgot all about the Maxwell and Sterling siblings.

The following night, Alexander had planned to take Stormy and me to the movies. *Night of the Living Dead* was showing at the downtown art theater, and it was one of my favorite movies. There wasn't much to do in Dullsville, and going to see a movie was a big deal for me. I'd get to sit next to Alexander and hold his hand in the darkness and pig out on popcorn while watching a scary movie. What more could a girl want?

I wandered around the upstairs hallway, waiting for Alexander to come down from the attic. I found Stormy waiting in her room, dressed in black jeans and a studded belt, with a ripped, dark blue shirt that had the word TRAGIC spelled out in red letters. She stood at the dresser and applied the final touches of stormy blue makeup to her eyes.

I watched in awe. What took most girls hours in front

of the mirror took only a few minutes for Stormy to do without a reflection to look at. She even applied burgundy lip liner and eggplant-colored mascara without so much as a smudge or mistake. She got ready and adjusted her outfit with such ease, I was greatly impressed. I wondered if I were a vampire how I'd ever manage to do such simple tasks without a mirror. I was sure to have makeup smeared around my face like a clown.

However, I did feel a tinge of pain in my stomach thinking that even though I, too, wanted to be a vampire, Stormy couldn't see how cute she was. She'd always been different in that way from every mortal girl, and I felt lonely for her.

She began brushing her jet-black hair when she spotted me standing by her doorway.

"Did you have a good time on your overnight—or over-day?" I asked.

"I had a blast!" Her eyes lit up as if she were Cinderella back from the prince's ball.

"You must still be exhausted from traveling and now dancing and hanging out with friends," I said. Phantom raced over to me and rubbed her head against my boot.

"I feel great," she responded enthusiastically.

"Where did you sleep?" I asked. I picked Phantom up and petted her.

"I shared a coffin with Luna. We talked most of the day."

I imagined the two girls as being inseparable. I bet they talked about Alexander, Romania, boys, and being vampires. I wish it could have been me.

"I bet that was fun," I said.

"I had the best time *ever.*"

I guess "ever" included our dinner last night. Or was I being paranoid? I had to give it more time for us to really connect. And to not be so competitive.

"It must be nice for the two of you to catch up," I said.

"Yes, I haven't seen her in a while. Especially since she was . . ."

"Yes?" I asked.

"Uh . . . turned."

"Is she much different?" I asked. I really wanted to know. It might be an indication of what I might go through someday.

"Oh yes."

I was hoping for that. In Luna's case maybe she wasn't as good a friend to her or she'd become more sinister.

"She's even more fun!" she exclaimed. "If you can imagine."

I mumbled quietly to myself.

"Well, I am glad you are here," I said. "Once I found out about you, I was dying to meet you."

"What do you mean once you found out?" she asked quizzically.

I'd just stuck my combat-shoed foot in my mouth. "I mean because Alexander is so cryptic. He didn't talk much about your family at first. I realized it was because he missed you all so much."

Stormy smiled, her purple and black bands glowing on

her teeth. She seemed pleased with my answer and to find out that Alexander was pained, too, by his leaving home. "Yes, it is very hard to get information from my brother. It's like pulling fangs."

"Well, let's go," Alexander said, coming down from his attic room and reaching me in the hallway.

Dullsville's artsy movie theater was really different from the suburban megaplexes. The theater and screen were dinky in comparison, and there was only one concession stand. However, it made the movie-viewing experience cozy and intimate. The seats were practically centuries old, red upholstered, and the floor was always still sticky from the popcorn and spilled drinks from the movie before.

Alexander bought his sister all the items she wanted—which was quite a lot. She tried to hold the supersized drink and popcorn, and it was almost impossible to see her behind them.

We walked into the empty theater. I was excited to sit in between them, or at least have Alexander in the middle, but Stormy squeezed between us both as we headed into the aisle. I wasn't sure if she was trying to separate us or hoped to be the one in the middle for the attention. I was actually flattered that she wanted to sit next to me. Either way, as the lights dimmed and the macabre music played, she and I stuffed our faces with popcorn, gummy bears, and submarine-sized colas. She even grabbed my arm a few times during the movie when the zombies marched after the mortals for their own feeding frenzy.

When the movie was over, she jumped up and asked to see it again.

"Another time and another day," Alexander said. "But we can see another zombie movie. They are killer."

We all headed to the car with smiles on our faces. When Alexander dropped me off, he finally gave me the kiss I'd been waiting for the whole night.

Instead of watching us or honking the horn, Stormy just sat in the front seat.

"Tomorrow she's all yours," Alexander said as he walked down the drive and blew me a last-minute kiss.

The following evening, I anxiously waited for Alexander to drop Stormy off at my house. She and I were going to have our own girls' night. Forget Luna Maxwell. Forget the Crypt. I was going to be hanging out with my boyfriend's sister. I wasn't sure how our evening was going to go—it could swing either way. Stormy and I could get along perfectly or she could find me a rival for the attention of her big brother. I'd never tried to impress anyone in Dullsville, and it was unlike me to be so concerned with what anyone thought about me, but I couldn't help wanting to have a great relationship with Stormy. I didn't know what to do to entertain her in a town that wasn't filled with excitement. We'd already gone to a movie and partied at the Crypt. I had Becky on speed dial in case I ran out of things to occupy her on my own.

I heard the sound of a car door shutting and raced down the stairs to open the front door.

Stormy sauntered up our front walk alongside Alexander. I could see a slight resemblance in their gait, pale features and dark locks, and gorgeous smiles.

Stormy appeared eager to arrive as she gave me a friendly wave. She looked sweet in black jean cutoff shorts, purple tights, and a V-neck, blood-red cardigan she wore backward, exposing the top of her petite back. A tiny purple Hello Batty backpack purse hung from her shoulders and rested slightly above her waist.

I winked at Alexander as Stormy entered my house. He gave me a quick "hello" kiss while she took a moment to examine our family room.

"I'll pick you up in a few hours," Alexander said. "Don't get into too much trouble," he said half seriously.

But Stormy was entranced with my house as if she'd never experienced a smaller-than-a-Mansion-type home.

I was reluctant to let Alexander leave. I loathed any time that we were apart when we *could* be together. But I reminded myself that I'd be in the company of the next-best thing, his little vampire sister.

"I'll come back later," he said. "Or if you guys go out, I can pick you up there, too. Just let me know."

Alexander gave me a quick kiss on the cheek and patted Stormy on the arm.

"Wow, this house is cute," she said when I closed the door.

"I guess you are used to mansions," I said.

"I like this better. It's not so lonely," she said under her breath, as if she hadn't even meant for me to hear.

Is that how the younger sibling felt at the Mansion and at their home in Romania? The vast expanse of an estate was not comforting but rather reinforced the physical space between herself and her family? I'd always wanted to be yards away from my family, so the thought of huge rooms and multiple places to hide seemed like a Barbie Dream House for me.

I heard my mom pulling her car into the garage.

That was quick, I thought. Billy Boy was upstairs tucked away in his hobbit hole, but I knew once my mother came in she'd dominate the conversation with her polite motherly banter.

I tried to continue to show Stormy around, but within a few moments, my mom was inside.

"I wasn't sure you'd be home," she said, holding several reusable bags filled with groceries. Then she noticed Stormy. "I didn't know you had company."

"Mom, this is Alexander's sister, Stormy. Stormy, this is my mom."

My mom set down her bags on our kitchen island and greeted Stormy. "Oh, it's so nice to meet you," she exclaimed.

"It's a pleasure to meet you, Mrs. Madison," the younger Sterling said. She extended her hand.

But instead of shaking it, my mom reached out and gave her a warm hug. "You can call me Sarah."

I grumbled inside. My mom had those swift moves that only a mother possessed. I couldn't have been so friendly to Stormy when I met her. But my mom—she filled the room with such positive maternal energy. And Stormy seemed to lap it up as she hugged my mom back as if she were her own.

"Have you both eaten dinner?" my mother asked. "I bought some frozen pizza. It won't take long to heat up."

"That is so kind of you, but I had dinner when I woke up," Stormy said.

My mom paused as if Stormy had misspoken.

"Uh . . . yes, we've both eaten," I said. "We're just going up to my room to figure out what we want to do."

"Well, it's so nice to meet you. How long will you be in town?" my mom asked.

"I hope for a while," she answered.

Stormy followed me up the staircase and ran her fingers against the banister.

"I'm sure there's tons of dust," I said.

"No, not really," she said as if she was disappointed.

"Wow—" she said as I showed her into my room. "This is cool."

My room was broody and moody even with the lights on. I couldn't take my dresser mirror down, nor my full-length one on the back of my door. So instead, to avoid any issues for Stormy, I had covered them with sheets. She didn't even mention it.

She was intrigued by the macabre decor and rummaged through my closets as if they were her own. I sat back and watched with ease at the genuine interest she displayed examining my things. It was only afterward that she thought she was being rude.

"I guess I shouldn't be doing this," she said. "Mother would kill me if she saw me acting this way."

"No, please, go ahead. It's really awesome to see

someone interested in my stuff."

"This is so fabulous. You have the best room."

"You think so? No one's ever said that," I admitted truthfully. Now, maybe Alexander liked my room—but no one else had complimented my decor.

"And my room at the Mansion is fabulous, too," she said with a grin.

"Do you really like your room there?" I asked. "I wasn't sure what you'd think of it."

"I do. No one has ever done something like that for me," she said, genuinely.

"Really?" I asked.

"Yes."

Not even Luna? I wanted to say. But I didn't want to bring up her name or hint that I might be envious of their prior friendship.

"I expected your room to be different somehow," she said.

"How do you mean?"

"Luna's room was really girlie."

There it was! Not a moment later. That name. I bit my lavender-stained lip.

"Like a fairy's room," she continued.

"I can only imagine it's really cool," I said, trying to hide any tension in my voice.

"Yes, it is very pretty."

I nodded my head and grinned.

"But yours is like what I'd want mine to be," she said.

"Really?" I asked, surprised.

"Yes, I mean, besides the one you decorated at the Mansion. I mean, this is what I like, too. I didn't expect you'd have a room that I'd want to have."

I wasn't sure what she meant, but I assumed it was a compliment.

"So what did you think it would be like?" I pressed, wanting more information from her.

"I'm not sure, really. I just didn't think it would be so cool."

That was the key to Stormy. I thought she didn't think she'd like Alexander's girlfriend—one that wasn't Luna. And now that she found we did have things in common, it wasn't something she'd expected.

Just then Nightmare darted into my room and jumped on my windowsill, curling up next to the curtain.

"You have a cat, too?" she asked.

"Yes, her name is Nightmare."

"She's so cute. Can I hold her?"

"Sure."

I scooped up my cat and petted her as I took her over to Stormy. "Alexander gave her to me. He found her in an old railroad car when she was a kitten."

I placed Nightmare in her arms. Stormy snuggled up to the black feline and caressed the bridge of her nose.

"I think she likes you," I said.

"I have Phantom, and you have Nightmare."

I could hear Nightmare softly purring. "I wonder if they'd get along."

"That would be cool to find out," I agreed. "I think Nightmare would love the Mansion."

Stormy played with Nightmare for a bit before she placed her back on the windowsill. "Can I look around some more?" she asked.

"Of course you can." I sat at my computer chair and watched as she held up outfits in front of herself. "You have some really awesome clothes. Where did you find this?"

She held up a three-quarter-length black-and-red knitted shirt.

"I got it at a thrift store and poked some holes in it."

"Fabulous!" she said. "I like this." She held up a black lace minidress. "I wish I had it."

I wasn't sure how to respond. No one had ever wanted to have something of mine, unless it was Billy Boy asking for computer paper.

"Uh . . . I think it might be a little big," I said. "But maybe—"

"I'm sorry. I shouldn't have said anything." She began putting it back. It was as if her mind had caught up to her mouth. She avoided eye contact, and she appeared slightly embarrassed.

"No—you can take it," I said. I had such trouble finding clothes in Dullsville that each outfit I did find meant something special to me. But this was the first time in my life that someone else appreciated them. "Please take it," I insisted. "I'm sure Jameson can find a tailor in town to fit it for you."

"You think?" she asked, excited, as if I'd given her a hundred dollars.

"Yes, I think it would look great on you."

"I can wear it to a dance," she said, modeling it.

Just then Billy walked by my door.

"Who's that?" she asked.

"My dopey brother."

"You have a brother?"

"Yes. Didn't Alexander tell you?"

"No."

"Has Alexander told you anything about me?" I pried, but Stormy now appeared more interested in my brother than hers as she continued to stare out the doorway.

"Can I meet him?" she asked.

"Billy?"

"Yes."

"But he's not cool like Alexander. He's a dork."

"I can't imagine a brother of yours who's a dork."

"Well, you don't have to imagine—you can see for yourself." I rose from my chair and headed for the doorway.

"Hey, Billy. Get in here," I called.

"I'm busy," he answered.

"There's someone I want you to meet."

When I didn't hear any movement, I said, "Excuse me" to Stormy, headed down the hallway, and pounded on Billy's door.

"I need to talk to you," I told him.

"I said I'm busy."

"I have someone I want you to meet."

"Me?" he asked skeptically. "Go away."

"No, really. It's Alexander's sister. Please be polite, for once."

He didn't respond.

"Open up, already!" I demanded. I was seconds from storming into his room and pulling him out by his ear.

But then he opened his door. "I'm the one in this house with manners," he snarled. "It's you who acts like you live in a zoo."

Billy finally came out of his room and followed me into mine. Stormy smiled brightly.

"This is Stormy," I said. "Stormy, this is Billy."

"It's a pleasure to meet you," she said, extending her hand. He wasn't sure what to do with the formality and finally shook it.

"Hi," he said. "I heard you were coming to town."

"Yes, I'm visiting my brother."

"Well . . . it was nice meeting you," he said.

There was an awkward pause between the two of them.

"Okay, thanks for saying hi," I said. "Now let's get back to the clothes and our plans for the evening."

Billy Boy returned to his room as Stormy continued to beam.

"Want to go to Hatsy's Diner for some shakes?" I asked her.

"Yes! And maybe Billy can come with us," she said.

"Uh . . . he's not into anything that doesn't involve microchips."

"Well, we'll just have to change that for next time," she said as we grabbed our things and headed out of the house.

Stormy was super impressed with the jukeboxes on the tables and the framed records on the walls. Conservative customers gawked at us, since we stood out like tombstones on a lawn. I was used to this treatment from my fellow Dullsvillians, but I felt protective of Alexander's sibling. I glared back hard at anyone who looked, and most turned back to their meals. Stormy was so caught up in the nostalgic restaurant that she didn't even notice.

"This is so American!" she said.

"Yes, I guess it is."

"I've seen places like this in movies."

"You can get anything you want," I offered.

"Do they have Romanian smoothies? Or steak tartare?"

"I don't think so. I think most things are cooked here."

"That's okay," she said. "I brought this with me just in case," she said. She pulled out a water bottle, only instead of water it appeared to be filled with blood.

Dixie, in her fifties-diner red-with-white-piping waitress uniform, shimmied her behind as she walked over to the table.

"What's that?" Dixie asked.

"Uh . . . it's Kool-Aid," I said.

"That doesn't look like Kool-Aid to me."

"It's an energy drink," Stormy tried to explain.

"Well, if you came here for a nutritious meal," Dixie said, "you came to the wrong place. If it's not fried, burnt, or floured, we don't serve it."

She chomped her gum and blew a bubble.

"No, we are indulging tonight," I said as Stormy surreptitiously slid her bottle back into her bag.

"Two chocolate malts, please," I said.

"That's all?" she asked.

"Yes. We just had dinner."

Dixie shimmied away, displeased that she didn't have a big order on her hands to increase her chances of a bigger tip.

We both laughed as she placed our order at the counter.

"This is fabulous," Stormy said.

"You think? I've been coming here for years with my best friend. Dixie has been working here since it opened."

Stormy flipped through the jukebox songs on our table.

"What is your favorite music?" I asked.

"I like the Skeletons."

"You do? So do I. I don't think they are on there. They only have fifties artists."

"What about Elvis?" she asked.

"Alexander loves him," I noted.

"I know. So do I."

I found a quarter in my pocket and placed it in the jukebox. "Play your favorite," I said. A moment later, "(Let Me Be Your) Teddy Bear" began to play overhead.

She seemed fascinated by the music and the power of her pushing the button and it playing.

Then I remembered the Sterlings lived by candlelight. Modern technology wasn't something they dealt with every day.

"So what's Alexander like as a big brother?" I asked. I was always dying to know more about my boyfriend— especially because he was so mysterious that I didn't even know until recently that he had a sister.

"He played with me when I was little, but when he got older, he went to his room most of the time and painted."

"What did you play?"

"Games mostly. He loved checkers, so I did, too. But when I pulled out my fashion dolls he ran for his room."

I laughed, and so did she.

"Do you always get along with him?"

"Yes, I guess so. I get on his nerves a lot," she said.

"I can't imagine that."

"Oh, it's true. When he and Luna were going to their ceremony—" Then she stopped. "I mean . . ."

"No, that's okay, you can tell me."

"I was dressed as the flower girl. I had dead black roses and held them in a small urn."

"I bet you were pretty," I said.

"Thank you. Luna was waiting for him to start the ceremony, and everyone was getting impatient. We couldn't find Alexander."

"Oh?"

"I was the one who found him sitting by himself outside a crypt. He told me that he wasn't going to the covenant altar with Luna. I got mad and poured the flowers on his shoes. And then I told my mother where he was."

I had never heard this story before, and from Stormy's point of view, Alexander's arranged eternal betrothal caused disappointment for many besides himself and Luna.

"I'm sure he understood." I tried to ease her guilt.

"When my mother got to the crypt, he was gone."

"What happened?"

"He eventually came home. But the Maxwells wanted revenge. Then he had to leave for Grandmother's Mansion here. But he didn't come back."

I didn't know what to say. "Well, you're together now," I said.

"Yes," she said. "Finally."

"What do you like to do?"

"I like to write poems."

"What about?"

"Boys."

"That's a great subject."

"I hope to have them published someday."

"I'm sure they will be," I assured her.

"I bet you are glad to see Jameson, too. He's so cool," I said.

"Yes, I've missed him. He's funny."

"Funny?" I asked.

"When I was little, he liked to hide my dolls during the day. So when I woke up, I'd have to search every room for them. I'd find them resting under the stairs, poking out from behind an antique vase, or sticking out from my coat pocket. It was a fabulous game."

I laughed, imagining Jameson sneaking around their Romanian mansion with dolls under his bony arms.

"He's a half vamp; that's why he can be out all day," she said.

"He is?" I asked.

"Yes, you didn't know?" She appeared surprised.

I didn't want to fib, but I also didn't want to appear like I hadn't been "in the know." "Uh . . ."

"Yes, he's mortal," she continued. "He can be out in day and night but needs a vein like we do to exist."

She said it so matter-of-fact that I was almost taken aback. I had to remind myself that I was, after all, sitting with a young vampire. But where Alexander was mysterious and kept much of this identity to himself, Stormy blurted out her information like any other girl without a secret.

"That's why I love his Romanian smoothies," she continued. "His California smoothies are terrible. They don't have blood."

"Blood?" a familiar voice said as someone scooted into the booth with me.

"What are you doing here?" I asked Trevor. Then he gazed at Stormy.

"Ditched Becky for the evening?" Trevor asked.

Dixie returned with our malts and placed them on our table. Trevor grabbed mine before I could and stuck my spoon in it. He took a scoop of my malt and put it in his mouth.

I wasn't about to be bullied in front of Stormy. It was uncomfortable enough for me to experience it without her having to experience it, too.

"That was Raven's," Stormy said forcefully. I was surprised that she was defending me. I was proud of her. She was feisty like I was. But ultimately I didn't want her to be involved in my torment.

"Raven likes to share," he said to her. "I didn't know you had a little sister," he said to me.

"I don't. This is *Alexander's* sister." I stressed Alexander, hoping that he'd pick up on not picking on her. That Alexander would seek revenge if he did. And that I'd stop him, too, if he tried.

"Oh . . . so Monster Girl has a Mini-Monster."

I was ready to dump the malt on his head, but I worried it wasn't the best example of proper behavior in front of Stormy. Instead I slid my hand underneath the table and pinched his leg with all my might.

"Ouch!" he said, putting the malt down.

I let go and gave him a death stare. "You can address her by her real name. Athena. Other than that, any name is a violation."

"A violation?" he chuckled.

"Yes, of Raven's law."

"I see. And if I break it, will you arrest me? Please?" He was as menacing as he was attractive. His blond hair flopped perfectly in place like a model's.

"It's time for you to go," I said. "Before you turn into a pumpkin."

"Fine," he said. "It was nice meeting you, Athena."

She extended her hand. He paused for a moment, surprised by her formality.

Then he shook her hand.

"Wow—you can learn a thing or two about manners

from her," he said to me.

"Uh . . . so could you."

Trevor walked off to the counter.

I pushed my malt away from me. I wasn't about to drink it.

"I'm sorry about that," I said. "He's been bugging me since he was born."

"I think he's cute!"

"Trevor?"

"Yes, this town is full of good-looking guys!"

"I think that's the jet lag talking," I said.

"He really likes you. That's why he picks on you," she said.

I was shocked by her keen insight into Trevor. "It's time to call Alexander," I declared.

Just then Dixie sashayed over and handed me another malt. "It's from Trevor."

"Ah," I said to Stormy. "I think your good manners are rubbing off on him."

A short time later, Alexander met us in the diner's parking lot. This time Stormy hopped in the back of the car.

"You can sit up front," I said.

"No, that's okay. I like being chauffeured," she said. I thought it was cute how she was slowly warming up to me.

"So, did you kids have fun?" Alexander teased.

"I did," I said.

"Yes, Raven gave me this dress," she said, pulling it out of the bag.

"You shouldn't be taking clothes from her," Alexander

scolded. Normally the driver looks in the rearview mirror when talking to the passenger in the backseat. But Alexander didn't. He knew he wouldn't be able to see his sister in the reflection.

"It's okay," I assured him. "I want her to have it."

"You've done enough already," he said.

"And I met her brother, Billy," Stormy added.

"That's cool. He's your age."

"I know . . ." Stormy giggled under her breath.

"Sounds like you guys had too much fun without me. I'm not sure you need me anymore."

"Of course we do," I said, putting my hand on his shoulder.

"Well, maybe not . . ." Stormy teased. I thought she liked the attention she was getting, no matter who it was from.

"And I met this guy named Trevor," she continued.

"You did?" Alexander asked. There was a hint of concern in his voice.

"It wasn't a big deal," I said.

"I think he likes Raven," she said.

Alexander paused.

"Are you trying to start trouble?" he asked.

"I'm just being honest."

"Well, he's going out with our friend Scarlet," I said. "Besides, Alexander doesn't have to worry about anyone."

"You should keep an eye on him," she warned Alexander. "I don't trust him."

"I have to keep my eyes on you," Alexander said. "One night out and you're already meeting boys and getting new dresses and hanging around the town bully."

Stormy giggled again. "Too bad you didn't come."

"Well, you've both had a full evening," he said, pulling into my driveway.

I stepped out of the car, and Stormy jumped out of the Mercedes, too. Instead of extending her hand to say good night, she smiled and leaned in to me. She wrapped her lithe arms around my waist and gave me a hug so hard I melted inside. Then she hopped into the front seat.

I was so flattered. I had had a great time, and so had Stormy.

Alexander took my hand and walked me to the door.

"I see you've made a good impression on her."

"I really had a blast," I said. "I wish I had a little sister."

We turned around and saw Stormy watching us from the car. I knew she was dying to see if her brother would kiss me.

She turned away like she hadn't been looking. She leaned over and got the dress out of the bag and began eyeing it instead.

Alexander took the now private opportunity and leaned in and kissed me. His lips were so tender that I became lost in them. Suddenly the car horn honked and we both jumped.

I tried to catch my breath, and Alexander was now frustrated with his sibling. Then we both burst out laughing.

"See, she's not so mannerly after all," my boyfriend said. "Thanks so much," he added as I unlocked the door. "This meant a lot to me."

"You don't have to thank me," I said truthfully. "I've been waiting for nights like these for all my life."

The following evening at dinner, I was chomping on grilled herb chicken when Billy asked out of the blue, "How long will Stormy be in town?"

"Why?" I wondered.

"The fall dance is coming up at school. I thought I could invite her."

I was stunned at my brother's suggestion. First, I couldn't imagine that my nerdy little brother had become brave enough to ask a girl to a dance, and two, the girl he wanted to be his date was a vampire.

"That would be so nice," my mom gushed. "I think you should."

"Sorry. No such luck," I said. "I think you should go, by all means, but you should ask one of your friends at school."

"Won't she be in town?" he asked. "It's this week."

I knew she'd be in town and I wasn't prepared to lie, even though it was the easiest solution.

"Uh . . . yes, she will be. But I don't think taking her would be a very good idea."

"Why not?" he asked.

"Yes," my dad said. "I think it's a great idea."

"Isn't there that girl from Math Club that you'd like to invite?" I asked. I remembered going to one of his parties at the library and seeing a girl there who appeared to be really attached to him.

"Yes, but I just thought it would be fun to ask Stormy."

"I'm dating Alexander. You can't date his sister," I said as if it were a fact.

"There isn't a law against it," he responded. "Besides, it's not a date. It's just a dance."

"This would be a wonderful opportunity for both of you," my mom said to Billy. "This will be Billy's first dance, and Stormy's first in America. She could learn a lot. I think it would be very special for them both."

Nerd Boy attending a school dance? I knew he was growing up, and if he'd been someone else's brother it might have been okay. But he was mine, and I knew his every smarmy quirk. I wasn't ready to accept he was growing up, and I definitely wasn't ready to see him falling for a vampire.

"I don't think so," I said. "Can we change the subject?"

"Why?" my mom pressed. It was just like her to get her nose into other people's business—especially mine.

Because she's a vampire, I wanted to say. But I knew I

couldn't share that information with them.

"She's Alexander's sister," I said instead. "And I don't want you to cramp my style."

"You don't have style!" my brother barked.

"Well, if you don't think I do, then why do you want to invite Stormy? She dresses like I do."

"Because . . ." he started, "I thought it was the nice thing to do."

I felt awful. It was really sweet of him to want to take Stormy to the dance. But I couldn't get past that he was my nerdy little brother.

Stormy was cool and cute. I could see why Billy Boy liked her, and I believed he genuinely did. But I had to think of a way out of the situation and ensure that Billy wouldn't want to take her to the dance.

"Well, if she goes, then I do, too," I threatened.

"I think that just killed the invite," my dad said.

"I thought so." I grinned like a chess champion.

"Fine," Billy said. "But bring Alexander, too."

My grin soured as I realized who was the champion after all. And it wasn't me.

"But she can't go!" I said to Alexander later that evening at the Mansion when I told him about Billy's invitation to the middle school dance. We were in his attic room while Stormy was being tutored by Jameson, who, I now knew, was in fact a half-vampire.

"Why not?" Alexander asked. "She'll be so excited."

"Because my brother is a nerd."

"He is not," Alexander said with a chuckle. "He's perfectly normal."

"And he doesn't know the truth about you and Stormy. That you both are vampires."

"I don't think that will be an issue."

"How can it not be?" I questioned worriedly. "He's very curious."

"Relax, Raven. It's just a dance. They'll be fine."

"There's one other problem," I began. I was hoping this would be the deal breaker that could shut the whole dance invite down. "I told Billy if he goes, so do I."

"You'll be his chaperone?" he asked.

"Uh . . . and so will you."

I was ready for everything to be called off right there and then. This was my excuse. I would tell Billy that Alexander refused to go.

But Alexander tilted his head and smiled brightly. "Okay," he said. "What should I wear?"

I was surprised that Alexander was game for us chaperoning. Instead of rolling his eyes, he seemed to like the idea that Billy wanted him to go, too.

"You want to go?" I asked, half whining.

"Sure. I think it will be fun."

"You're not worried about your sister going to a dance with a bunch of mortals?"

"No, I think it would be good for her. I like the solitude of the Mansion. But Stormy, she's not like me. She needs to be social as much as she needs to drink blood."

I wasn't expecting Alexander to be so excited about

the fall dance. I thought if he wasn't game, we'd be able to get out of it, thus blocking Billy from taking Stormy. Since I loathed the idea of going to my brother's school dance, I felt torn. I would much rather be running around tombstones than chaperoning a dance, but going anywhere with Alexander was better than not being with him at all.

"All right," I said. I couldn't imagine that my brother and I would both be on the arms of vampires. "But no one gets bitten unless it's me."

Later that night, Alexander and I arrived at the Crypt. I preferred dancing at the club to my brother's school gymnasium.

I was bopping on the dance floor while Alexander was talking to Sebastian when Jagger spotted me as he headed to the bar.

"So . . ." Jagger said. "You really like it here, do you?"

"I love it. I have to admit, despite your history with Alexander, you really do have talent," I said, and stepped off the dance floor to talk to him and catch my breath.

"You think so?" he asked, his white hair cascading over his blue and green eyes.

"Look at this. You have all of Dullsville High here. They love it."

"But you do, too?" he asked with a mischievous and playful grin.

"I love it the most. Are you kidding?"

"Why?" he asked in a serious and deliberate tone.

"Why do you think you belong with us more than your own kind?"

"It's just who I am. That's all that I can say. I was born this way."

"And I was, too. I'm surprised Alexander didn't turn you the first moment he saw you. I would have."

Jagger's back was to Alexander, but I could see my boyfriend keeping a watchful eye on us from across the room.

"What do you mean by that?" I asked.

"He's a vampire. It's enough to prey upon a young mortal—but to have one willing? It's a travesty not to take advantage of the situation."

"Well, that's where you both are different."

"He's not like us," Jagger said with intensity.

"He's not like anyone. That's why I love him."

"But there are others you can be with. Others who can make your wish come true. At the Coffin Club. Here."

I didn't like Jagger insinuating anything about my relationship with Alexander, or that I'd consider being turned by anyone else.

"But it doesn't matter—just as long as it's with Alexander."

"Really," he said. "Is that what you feel down in your soul? You said you were born this way. That was a long time before you met Alexander. Don't you wonder about what you are missing?"

I knew what I was missing. But I had to be patient.

"What are you waiting for?" he asked.

Just then Alexander appeared. There was a truce

between the two, but he glared at his former nemesis. Alexander wasn't too possessive of me—and he didn't need to be. I wasn't the kind who flirted with just anyone. But I could tell there was an underlying mistrust of the Maxwells that went as deep as blood.

I wanted Billy to have a positive experience for his first dance, and I wanted to make sure he'd treat Stormy to the gentlemanly behavior that Alexander always showed me. I didn't want my brother to act like the Nerd Boy that he was, so I brought in reinforcements—my mother.

She dragged us both to Jack's Department Store, and while she was outfitting Billy with a new suit, I browsed through the junior dresses. I had already decided on a dress at home, but I saw one on the clearance rack that caught my eye. It was a stunning strapless indigo-blue corset dress with hints of black feathers. Wow—I never found things like this in Dullsville, only during Halloween or at a thrift store.

I took it off the rack and quickly read the size—which happened to be mine. I held it up to me and felt exhilarated.

I checked out the price. It had been marked down several times. *Who wouldn't want this?* I thought. But then I saw a few girls examining the dresses that weren't marked down. And then I knew. It wasn't their style, and it wasn't *full* price. I took the dress back to the guys' department to show my mom.

I didn't recognize my brother at first. There was a young man in a suit in front of the mirrors outside the changing room. My mom was fussing over him and trying to make sure the length of his pants was just right. I couldn't believe that the handsome young man was the boy who had bugged me all my life.

I was surprised at how grown up my brother looked wearing dress pants and a sport coat. I gave him a thumbs-up, and he appeared pleased by my fashion affirmation.

I showed my mom the dress I'd picked out. "It's on sale," I said. "Can I get it?"

"It's beautiful," she said. "Where did you find it?"

"In the juniors. It's my size, too." I showed her the price.

"We'll take both," my mom said cheerfully to the salesman.

"It's that time of year," he said. "Fall dances."

My mom was overjoyed as the salesman rang up our purchases. "I never thought I'd see this day," she said joyfully. "Both of you going to a dance, and it being the same one."

"Neither did I," my brother and I said in unison.

* * *

The three of us went to our local florist to pick out a small wrist corsage for Stormy. Dullsville's florist shop was a family-owned one-room store with a huge display of flowers, vases, and knickknacks. A friendly woman wearing a pink-and-green-striped apron was finishing up with another customer.

"I'll be right with you," she said.

Billy looked lost in the jungle of flowers without his cell, computer, or video games, clearly bored.

"I don't even know what she is wearing," he said when I showed him a few flowers.

Good point, I thought.

"May I help you?" the florist asked, coming over to us.

"We'll need a small wrist corsage," my mom said. "For a school dance."

"What color would you like?" she asked.

Billy shrugged his shoulders. "Do you have something black?" Billy asked.

The florist looked at Billy like he was deranged.

"You are going to a dance, not a funeral," my mom teased. "How about pink?"

Billy shook his head. "I'm not sure she'd like that." Billy looked to me for help.

"I know she likes purple," I told him.

"Yes, that's what I want," he said emphatically. "Purple."

The florist showed us several purple flowers. Billy was overwhelmed with which one to pick and turned to my mom and me for guidance. We narrowed them down, and Billy was still uncertain which one to choose. Floral arranging was out of my twelve-year-old brother's skill set.

"It's okay," I said. "They are all beautiful."

That gave Billy the confidence he needed, and he pointed to one to make the final decision.

The florist placed some baby's breath around it and began to prepare it for a corsage.

"How much longer?" Billy asked. I could tell he'd rather have been home playing Warcraft.

"This will all be worth it," I said, "when you see the look on her face."

That night Billy descended the staircase in his suit. I was already waiting in my new corset dress, so excited to have something new to wear in front of Alexander.

I hated to admit that my pesky brother did look handsome when he came down the stairs in his navy suit.

"Whose brother are you?" I teased.

"Not yours," he quipped.

"You look terrific," my dad said proudly.

"You look gorgeous," my mom gushed. Billy tensed up as my mom straightened his collar.

"Get off," he snarled.

"I just need to adjust this," she said. Then she took his chin and squeezed it. "You look so grown up."

"Mom—" he said.

"We have to go," I said, helping him out of the parental trap.

"Wait—let me get a picture of you both," she said.

"No, Mom," he whined. "We have to go."

"I need memories!" she exclaimed. "For my scrapbook."

My mom grabbed her camera. "Get together," she said, gesturing for us to stand next to each other. We both moved like slugs.

"C'mon. It won't kill you to take one picture," my dad commanded.

Reluctantly, we stood side by side. I hadn't noticed that Billy was nearly as tall as I was. In no time he'd be towering over me.

"Smile," she said.

Billy and I grimaced.

"Smile, already!" she repeated.

"Okay," we both said through grinning, gritted teeth.

The flash burst, and we were both momentarily blinded.

"One more," she directed.

"You said only one." Billy was itching to go.

"But what if that doesn't turn out?" she asked.

"Then you'll know that one of us is a vampire," I said.

Billy headed for the door while I grabbed my sweater.

"Knock 'em dead tonight," my dad said.

I couldn't tell him that our dates were, in fact, *un*dead.

"I was hoping I'd get to meet Stormy, too," my dad added.

"That's what happens when you have a son," I said, opening the front door.

My dad let me borrow the car, and we headed over to the Mansion. I was hoping that Billy would chicken out

upon arriving at the haunted-looking house, but he didn't.
I think since he was with me he felt more at ease, or maybe
he felt like he was becoming a man or something.

I made him knock on the door.

Jameson opened it slowly, like in a creepy silent movie.
Billy was as nervous seeing Jameson as he was for his date.
I couldn't help but feel anxious for him.

I put my hand on Billy's shoulder. "I know she'll be
happy to see you," I said.

He turned back to me like I'd said the kindest words
anyone had ever said to him. At once, he stood up a little
straighter and appeared at ease.

"Good evening, Mr. Billy," Jameson said.

"Good evening, Jameson," Billy said proudly.

"Please come in. I know Miss Athena is almost ready."

"Who is Athena?" Billy whispered to me.

"That's Stormy's real name," I replied.

"Oh. That's really pretty."

Just then Alexander came down the stairs. He was so
hot in his dark jacket and silken dress pants, I could feel my
knees quiver just catching sight of him. I couldn't believe
that someone so handsome was indeed my boyfriend. His
face brightened when he saw me.

"You look beautiful," he said.

He came over and gave me a tender kiss on the cheek.
I wanted to swoon into his arms and have him carry
me away. I had to remind myself that this was Billy and
Stormy's dance and not mine.

Stormy descended the creaky old staircase in the dress

I'd given her. The black corset minidress had sheer lace sleeves that just covered her pale shoulders and ruffled black and purple lace that made up the skirt. She wore knee-high black tights and witchy boots with purple lace-ups that matched the ties and lacing on her corset. Her hair was up in a small bun with several curls cascading down her cheeks. She was radiant.

Billy politely handed her the flower box.

"For me?" she asked sweetly.

"Yes, we picked it out just for you," Billy answered, his voice quavering slightly.

Stormy opened it, and her eyes lit up. "It is beautiful!" she said.

Billy shifted in his stance, a huge smile on his face.

I helped her get the corsage out of the box and slipped it on her wrist.

"And I have something for you, too," Alexander said to me. He grabbed a small box off of the hallway table. "I hope you like it."

I opened it to find a brilliant blue flower. "It totally matches my dress!" I said. I gave him a quick kiss. "It's perfect. How did you know?"

"I had a little help from a friend," he replied.

My brother smiled proudly.

I took it out of the box and tried my best to pin it on my dress.

"Here, let me help you," Alexander said.

"Don't prick your finger—" I said. "Or more importantly, mine."

Stormy and Billy watched as Alexander did his best not to draw blood out of either one of us.

Jameson opened the Mansion door for us and we piled into the car. As Alexander drove us to the dance, I hoped Billy didn't catch sight of his date missing in the rearview mirror.

When we arrived at Dullsville Middle, Billy hopped out of the car and opened the door for Stormy. Alexander and I eagerly followed the pair into the building. Stormy wore my dress proudly; it fit her like a doll. She was beautiful and held her head high as she walked into the school next to Billy.

The middle school appeared the same as when I went there and when I'd visited it to meet Henry for the first time. Posters, signs, and handmade art peppered the hallways. Immediately we got stares from shocked attendees. We weren't following typical Dullsville student dress code—me in my corset dress, Stormy in hers, and Alexander in his tailored, million-dollar dark silk suit. Billy looked in place, but the students and faculty eyed his strange entourage.

Stormy seemed to glow in the school hallway. She responded like Alexander had when I'd brought him to Dullsville High for the first time. Since both Sterlings were homeschooled, they missed even the most mundane and minute things about school—a drinking fountain, a pep rally sign, a cafeteria. I'd have given all those things away for a coffin bed and a life without the sun. But I watched as

Stormy took in the sights and smells of her new surroundings.

Billy did his best to overcome his shyness. He showed Stormy every inch of the school as if he were the school administrator. I was secretly proud of my brother. He treated Stormy as a gentleman would, opening doors for her and, once they were inside the gymnasium, offering her a drink.

The gymnasium was slightly transformed from a basketball court into the middle school's fall dance. Leaves decorated the walls alongside GO, EAGLES banners. A long table held refreshments—bottled water, sodas, and juices—while another one had baskets filled with snacks. A dozen more cafeteria tables with plenty of seats lined the dance floor, and a DJ spun a slow love song.

What I hadn't anticipated were girls who seemed threatened by Stormy's presence. Especially the girl I'd once seen at a Math Club party. She stared at Alexander's sister with a jealous glare.

No one was out on the dance floor. Instead, all the students were sitting at the tables or hanging out by the snack area. Most of the girls were talking to other girls, and the guys were clustered together with their friends.

"I haven't been to many school dances. Is this what it's really like?" I asked Alexander.

"I don't know," he said. "I don't even go to school."

We both laughed.

"Why isn't anyone dancing?" Stormy asked Billy.

He shrugged his shoulders.

"Are we going to dance?" Stormy asked.

"Uh . . . sure." He pulled awkwardly at his tie. "But maybe we should wait for a bit until some others start."

Stormy tapped her witchy boot impatiently on the wooden floor. Then, all at once, she boldly grabbed Billy's hand and pulled him out to the middle of the gymnasium.

My brother was horrified. He stood alone with his odd date in the center of a hundred peers' watching eyes. I actually felt bad for him. I was afraid he'd freak out—run off the dance floor or even faint.

Whispers echoed throughout the gym. And then students started to laugh.

Billy watched as his classmates sneered at him and his date. His face flushed red. I guessed at any moment he'd hightail it out of there and we'd have to take a tearful Stormy home.

But Billy didn't leave. Instead, he took Stormy's hand and placed his other hand around her waist. She smiled with delight, and he returned a flashy grin. Before I knew it, he was slow dancing with Alexander's little sister.

A tear welled in my eye as I saw my brother dance bravely with a girl in front of the entire school. It was so weird watching my little pesky brother holding a beautiful girl in his arms. The two moved back and forth, not always in time with the music, but nevertheless together. Stormy leaned her head on his shoulder and the tear ran down my cheek. Then several more Dullsville Middle School students raced onto the dance floor as if they'd been waiting for some courageous soul to start the night off. Within a few minutes a dozen couples had joined Billy and Stormy. The music changed to an upbeat dance tune and even more students joined in.

Alexander turned to me. "Getting misty on me?" he said. "I guess you can't hide your fondness for the little guy."

Embarrassed, I wiped the tear from my face and patted my mascara and eyeliner in hopes that they weren't going to run.

"Want to dance?" Alexander asked. "I can't let my sister have all the fun."

"Of course!" I exclaimed.

Alexander took my hand and led me onto the dance floor. The younger students smiled at us as they, too, bobbed to the high-spirited music. Alexander spun me around, and I was so dizzy from spinning and being in his company that I forgot where we were. My handsome boyfriend gazed down at me with all the love I'd ever seen from one person. He drew me close and kissed me with such passion that I thought I'd gone to heaven.

When we stopped kissing, we looked up to see all the students' and faculty's eyes on us. Several teachers and other chaperones cleared their throats and shot us dirty looks. Then the students cheered and applauded us. I beamed proudly while Alexander grinned awkwardly.

Several of Billy's nerdmates came up to him and Stormy

and talked and danced the night away. I sat back, watching my baby brother score the popularity I never had with my peers.

When the dance was over, Alexander and I walked our siblings out to the car. I watched as Billy again held the door open for Stormy. It was as if he had come into the dance a boy and came out a young man. Billy was beaming, displaying more confidence than I'd ever seen in him.

"That was so much fun!" Stormy said as we drove home.

"Yeah, and the best part was when our chaperones almost got kicked out for making out on the dance floor!" Billy exclaimed.

Our siblings laughed while Alexander and I tried to cover our embarrassment.

"I want a picture of us together, Stormy," Billy said when we pulled up to the Mansion. "Raven, you can take it with my cell phone."

My heart broke a little then. It was Billy's first dance, and he wouldn't have a picture of his date. I wasn't sure what to say.

We all climbed out of the car.

"I don't like pictures," Stormy said.

"But why?" Billy asked. "You're so pretty."

She blushed ruby red.

Billy stood next to Stormy and tossed me his phone. "Take it," he commanded.

Stormy was still glowing from Billy's compliment.

I looked to Alexander for help. But the pair appeared so happy, neither one of us wanted to be the ones to break their spell.

Alexander shrugged his shoulders and I quickly snapped one picture and tossed it back to Billy. He checked it and stared at it oddly.

Stormy tapped him on the shoulder, distracting him from the camera.

"Good night, Billy. I had a great time," she said sincerely.

"I did, too," he said.

Stormy gave him a quick kiss on his cheek as Jameson opened the door for her.

My brother's face illuminated like a *Star Wars* lightsaber.

Stormy waved to him as he headed to our car to wait for me. Alexander gave me a long good-night kiss and I, too, was buzzing from our magical evening.

As I drove away, Billy stared back at the looming Mansion like I had many times, gazing at it until it disappeared as we turned the corner.

"So, did you have fun?" I asked.

"The best night of my life." He stared out the window with a huge, boyish grin.

For once, Billy and I agreed on something. There was no better time than that spent with the Sterlings. I was hoping Billy didn't get too attached to Stormy, though. If someone in the Madison household was going to be turned into a vampire, I had first dibs.

I was really proud of my brother. I'd always been

the risk taker, the one who did things against the grain. Though he was more conservative, I realized now that when pushed, he, too, could be fearless. It must have been in our blood.

10

Starry Night

After the night of the dance, Stormy was dying to see Billy again, and though our younger siblings were clearly old enough to spend time by themselves, Alexander was mindful of his little sister in a foreign country. So on their next adventure together, a few evenings later, Alexander and I followed close behind.

We went to Evans Park, where Billy, Henry, and Stormy hung out by the swings while Alexander and I sat atop the hill. The park was the one Becky and I frequented, with a swing set, a run-down tennis court, and lush grassy areas for picnics or hanging out. We were all eyeing the stars; Billy and Henry were showing off Henry's telescope, and Alexander and I were lying on a blanket gazing at the sky as we held hands.

But the star that most intrigued me was my own

boyfriend, whose handsome face was only a few inches from mine.

I continued holding his hand and softly stroked his lean, strong arm. I still couldn't get over how lucky I was to have Alexander in my life. He was everything I wanted in a guy; when he was in my company, I had to touch him to make sure that he was in fact real.

We took the opportunity to share some kisses privately. His lips were always as tender as imaginable.

I heard the trio talking down by the swings, but I couldn't make out their conversation.

"I wonder how our lives would have been if I'd met you when we were younger," I said, staring into Alexander's dreamy chocolate-colored eyes.

"Like when you were in middle school?" he asked, knotting his fingers around mine.

"Yes. Wouldn't that have been cool?"

"Or when we were kids. We could have played in the sandbox together. I could have pulled your hair."

"And I could have pulled yours," I said with a laugh. "Would you have liked me then?" I asked. "I know I would have had a crush on you."

"Really?" he asked. "Even then? Even if you didn't have to sneak into my house and check out the new guy in town?"

"Uh . . . I was sneaking in that house for years," I said. "Of course I would have snuck in if you'd moved there earlier. Think about it. We'd have had so much more time together."

"Yes, but I am happy that I met you at all."

"Me too!" I leaned in and gave him a juicy kiss. "I bet you were so hot when you were twelve." I stroked his face. "But you didn't go to middle school, did you?" I asked.

"I never went to school."

"Did you go to dances?"

"No, there was not a school to dance in. Just my house."

"You mean mansion."

"Uh . . . I guess."

"So how did you meet girls?"

"When I went out with Sebastian, when we traveled, and when we hung out with other vampire families."

"And Stormy? How does she make friends and meet boys?"

"She has friends. But this is really a big deal to her. She is isolated, like I was. But she likes to be out with people."

"And you don't?"

"Well, certain people," he said, giving my hand a squeeze. "But I can spend my nights painting. She'd rather be out dancing. That's why I think it's good that she's getting out here. She has such a passion for life."

"And guys," I said with a grin. Then my mood changed. "What if she really likes Billy?" I asked.

I imagined my brother as a vampire: spending his long nights holed up on the computer instead of running around a cemetery, and sleeping in a remote-controlled coffin with more gadgets than a souped-up car.

"I think that's something we don't have to worry about

now. It's just one night. And you don't want him to be a vampire, do you?" he asked.

"Vampires are sexy. Not nerds."

Alexander laughed, his face lighting up in the night sky.

"Besides, I'm the one in the Madison family that will be turned."

"Oh," he said. "And when will that happen?"

"Sooner than later, please," I pleaded. I pulled my hair away from my neck and nuzzled up to him. "How about now?"

Just then we heard a girl's scream. We both sat up.

Stormy was walking away from Billy and Henry and heading toward us.

"What's going on?" I asked as Alexander and I rose.

"Nothing," Stormy said with a huff. "But I think we should go."

"What happened?" Alexander asked.

"Did they hurt you?" I asked. "I'll—"

"No, of course not," she said sweetly.

"Then what happened?" Alexander asked.

"It's nothing, really. I just think it's time to go."

I marched down to my brother and his nerdmate. I knew I'd get answers from him.

By this time Billy and Henry were putting pieces back in his telescope.

"What did you do?" I charged.

"Nothing," Billy said, perplexed.

"We were just fixing the telescope," Henry said.

"Something must have happened," I insisted. "I heard her scream."

"I don't know," Billy said. "We were just fixing the telescope and wiping down the mirror. Henry flashed it at her as a joke, and she freaked out!"

Oh, I thought. *Not that.*

"What's the big deal?" Billy asked.

"I don't know," I said.

"It didn't even touch her," Henry said sincerely.

"I know," I reassured him. "You didn't do anything wrong."

"We were just going to look at the stars," Billy said, shaking his head. "You goth girls! I think I'll stick to hanging out with the girls in Math Club. They aren't so weird."

"It's okay," I said.

"What girl is afraid of mirrors?" Billy asked.

"A vampire, I suppose," Henry said.

Billy looked back at me. He gazed at Stormy and Alexander for a bit. Then he took the mirror from Henry and slipped it into his pants pocket.

"Hey," Henry said. "I need that."

I glared at my brother. "It's time we go," I said, and shook my head as they packed up their belongings.

"Do you think Stormy will be okay?" I asked Alexander outside my house after we dropped the boys off at Henry's.

"She's fine. It's just one of the tricky parts of hanging

out with mortals," Alexander said with a cute grin.

I glanced back to check on Stormy, but this time she wasn't watching us from the car. Instead she was fiddling with the car radio.

"I feel awful," I said. "I didn't know they'd do that."

"There wasn't any way to know. And she could have shrugged it off. Instead she had to act all medieval."

"I guess I would have done the same."

"Well, if you are to become one of us, you will have to get used to such things," he said, guiding my hair back off my shoulder. "And by acting crazy, you just draw attention to it. Now we have to think of something to say to your brother."

Alexander was right. If I were a vampire, things would happen in the normal world to expose my true identity. I wasn't sure if I'd be as calm and cool as Alexander or more emotional like Stormy. For some reason, I feared I was more like the vampire girl sitting in the Mercedes.

But for now, I didn't have to worry about my reactions, only Stormy's. I guess it could have been anything that set her off. And maybe it was better that something happened now rather than later. Before our siblings got any closer.

Alexander and I decided it might be a good idea to keep Billy and Stormy apart from each other for a few days. But that didn't stop Billy from asking about her. He'd pass me in our upstairs hallway and ask how she was doing. I knew my brother truly felt bad. He'd taken her to a dance and they both had a great time, and now he felt he'd ruined her stay in Dullsville.

"She's not mad," I said to him one night at dinner. "Maybe she has a fear of mirrors."

"Well, she shouldn't. You'd think someone as pretty as her would be looking in them all the time."

It was one of Billy's first experiences with girls, and I didn't want him to be soured by them just because one was a vampire. But there was no way I could have told him or even avoided the situation, because I hadn't known that they'd be retooling the telescope. In fact, I didn't even know there was a mirror inside it.

The following night, I was waiting for the sun to set outside the Mansion when I came upon an object lying at the top of the front stairs. On closer inspection, it appeared to be a bouquet of flowers. I held the flowers and smelled them as the sun set behind me. When it was dusk, I rapped on the serpent knocker. Jameson opened the door, and I handed him the bouquet. "They were lying here on the steps," I said.

He looked at the card. Just then Stormy hopped down the stairs.

"Hi, Raven," she said.

"Hi, Stormy."

"This is for you, Miss Athena," Jameson said.

Her dark eyes lit up.

"Are they from you, Raven?" she asked.

"No," I said. "I found them on the stoop."

"Perhaps they are from a secret admirer," the Creepy Man teased with a toothy smile.

She looked at three purple carnations wrapped in baby's breath. "They're so pretty," she cooed.

Alexander came down the staircase in a tight pair of black jeans and a white T-shirt, his hair still slightly damp from showering.

"I got a bouquet of flowers," Stormy said, rushing to him.

"From Raven?" Alexander asked.

"No," I said again. I was starting to feel bad that they weren't from me.

Alexander tried to snatch the card.

"No—it's mine," Stormy said, and hurried into the formal living room and flung herself down on the sofa.

"Read it out loud," Alexander said as we followed her. "We're all dying to know."

She took out the card. *"Hope when you see the stars you think of us—in a good way.*

Sincerely, Billy and Henry'"

Wow. I didn't know my brother had it in him.

Stormy batted her glittery eyelashes. She was really touched by the gesture.

She didn't have to say a word. Her expression was that of a smitten girl who was touched to have received flowers from two boys.

"We shall put them in a vase," Jameson said.

"Yes, we must!" Stormy said. She jumped off the sofa

and quickly headed for the kitchen as the butler followed slowly behind her.

I could tell Stormy was feeling lonely for people her own age. But I also knew she liked my brother and his friend.

"That was really cool of your brother," Alexander said. "Maybe it's best for now that I keep her busy here?"

But keeping them apart was as bad as forcing two people together. We needed to let Stormy make her own decision.

Stormy returned with the vase of flowers. "I'm going to put them in my room," she said, but then stopped before she reached the staircase. She spun around and came over to me. "Do you think Billy will be going to the haunted house at the Crypt? Luna told me all about it."

"No," I said, not imagining my brother stepping foot in the Crypt. "I think he and Henry are going trick-or-treating."

"Oh . . ." she said, disappointed. She sighed like a deflating balloon. "I was hoping I could see him there."

She started for the stairs once more, then doubled back again to me. "Uh . . . do you think? I know it's rude to ask."

"No, go ahead," I said, putting my hand on her shoulder.

"Do you think I can go trick-or-treating instead?"

"You'd rather do that than go to the Crypt?" Alexander asked.

"We practically live in a haunted house," she said with

a laugh. "I can see that every day. Besides, I'd like to hang out with Billy and Henry. Please?"

I looked to Alexander for his approval.

"If Billy and Henry say it's okay," he replied. "You'd probably have more fun with them."

"I think those flowers are your answer," I said, "but I'll check with him for sure."

Naturally, Halloween was one of my favorite times of the year. I wish it could have been celebrated three hundred and sixty-five days a year. I'd never grow tired of it, as it seemed as if everyone in town was in a good and giving mood.

Jagger had closed part of the Crypt for a few days so he could fix it up for the haunted house, but the dance floor was open. A few nights later, Alexander, Stormy, and I headed over.

We were getting ready to hit the dance floor when I spotted Jagger. I waved him over.

"So when can we see what you are up to?" I asked Jagger. I was longing to get any information about it that I could before Halloween night came. I wanted to be in the know.

"You'll see on Halloween," he said with a sultry voice. "And not a day before. You want to be scared, don't you?"

"Will it be open to everyone?" I asked.

"You mean you? Or vampires?"

"I mean all of us."

"It will be open to the locals. I think that includes you. Will you be coming?" he asked Stormy.

"I'm hoping to go trick-or-treating," she said.

"What? You have to come here and see me!" Luna said.

"I know," she said. "But I'm going trick-or-treating with some friends."

"Friends?" she asked. "And who would they be?"

"Uh, just some kids I met." It was unclear why she wasn't telling Luna who they were. I figured perhaps because one of them was my brother and she didn't want Luna to feel competitive with me.

"Well, if you're not coming to the Crypt, then we should at least shop together and help pick out Halloween costumes."

"But what about Raven?" Stormy asked.

"Raven? I'm not sure that's a good idea. She'd be a third wheel," she whispered.

Stormy squirmed. I could tell she was struggling with including me in her and Luna's adventure.

"I think we vampire girls should stick together," Luna said, her pink lips triumphantly stretching across her porcelain face.

Stormy took a breath and looked up at Luna. "I think it will be fun to shop together, but I want to go with Raven as well."

Luna's smile turned into a frown. She was stunned by Stormy's declaration. "Well," she said, "I think we'll talk more about this later," she said. "I have to go see Romeo." Then Luna spun away from us and headed to the bar.

"I didn't mean to hurt her feelings," Stormy said, looking at me. "I was just being honest."

"I think she'll get over it," I said, secretly knowing she wouldn't.

11

Prada-Bees

The following day at school, the students were abuzz about Jagger's haunted house.

"Jagger is going to have a haunted house at the Crypt. I can't wait. I know it will be a real scream!" I heard a Prada-bee say in the hallway.

"I know I'll faint for sure," her friend squealed as they grabbed books from their lockers.

"Well, maybe Trevor can catch you," another teased.

"Don't you know?" the first girl, Heather, asked. "He's been hanging out with that skank—the one with over-dyed scarlet hair and tattoos instead of jewelry."

"Oh yes, that's old news. But I was hoping it wasn't true. You know how he is. Fixated on Raven. I think he likes that new girl just so he can feel like he's dating her."

"Nuh-uh!" the first one said.

"Yes."

"What do you think you'll go as?"

"I don't know. I really didn't have an idea for this year."

"We should go as Raven," the first one said loud enough for me to hear.

"What?"

"We can get tattoos and streak our hair."

"Gross!"

"And wear black lipstick."

"We'll look like we're dead."

"Isn't that the point? It's Halloween."

The second one sighed. "Trevor seems to be, like, in love with her."

"I wonder how he'll feel about *me* if I dress like her."

"You think?"

"He likes Raven. He keeps dragging that scarlet-hair chick to games. I think he really digs that look."

"That look—or *Raven's* look."

"Whatever. You want to go out with Trevor, don't you?"

"Duh!"

The first one took her friend's affirmative answer as motivation and headed to me.

Becky and I were grabbing textbooks from our locker.

"Hi, Becky," the first one said.

"Hi, Becky," the other said.

"Hi, Heather," Becky responded politely. "Hi, Courtney."

"Uh, Raven," Heather began. "Where do you get your clothes?"

"Off of dead people?" Courtney mumbled with a laugh.

"Ssh!" Heather said to her. "No, really, I want to know."

I wasn't sure what to say. I knew on the one hand they were trying to make fun of me. And then on the other hand, if they wanted to see how the other half lived, they might actually like it.

"We want to go goth this year. Any hints?" Heather continued.

I didn't want to divulge my secrets to them. They wore what they did to be "in." I wore what I did because it was me. It was my soul. It was my being.

Last year I went as a tennis player. And a tennis player should be able to dress as a goth. It was, after all, Halloween.

But I didn't feel like making it too easy on them.

"You can go to the thrift store," I told them. "I think they should have something black that you can rip up and make look really funky." I was pleased with myself that I gave them some helpful tips.

"Ooh," Heather said. "Wear something someone else has worn?"

"Not in this lifetime," Courtney added.

I rolled my eyes.

Just then Trevor turned the corner.

"Hi, Trev!" Heather said to him.

Trevor was passing out orange flyers with black

writing. He handed them each one, and they read them to themselves.

"This looks like fun," Courtney flirted. "We'll see you there?"

"Oh, you'll see me, all right, but you may not recognize me." The two girls giggled and then headed back to their lockers. Then he looked at me. "You don't need a flyer," he said. "You already know."

"I'd still like to have one," I insisted.

His gaze was cute but menacing. "For your scrapbook of horrors?"

"Yes, right next to my picture of you."

I snagged a flyer from his hand before he took off.

Becky and I read it.

HAUNTED HAPPENINGS
LEAVE YOUR FEARS AT THE DOOR
BE THE FIRST TO MAKE IT OUT ALIVE
DATE: THIS SATURDAY NIGHT
LOCATION: THE CRYPT

"I will be clinging to Matt for dear life!" she said.

"And I'll cling to Alexander."

"But you aren't afraid of anything," Becky teased.

"Well, I still can cling to him, can't I?" I said with a wink.

"Can he see in the dark?" she whispered. "Or does he have night vision?"

"Yes, he can see."

"How cool! I knew he had superhuman powers."

"He'll be my hero for the evening. He can save us all from the creepy monsters!"

Becky looked at me as if to say, "Why should I be scared of a guy dressed up as a ghost when I'm standing by a real vampire?"

"Believe me," I said. "It's Jagger's haunted house. It will be scary—even for a vampire!"

Becky and I screamed out loud, then giggled until we couldn't breathe while the Prada-bees shot us looks like we were insane.

Shortly after sunset, Becky and I picked up Stormy and we headed over to our seasonal Halloween store, which had a great selection of costumes. Scarlet and Onyx were waiting for us inside.

"Is Luna coming?" I asked. I knew Stormy wanted her to be a part of the group. But Luna had made it clear at the Crypt that she insisted that it be the two of them only, and that left Stormy with a difficult choice.

"No," Scarlet said. "I told her to come, but she seemed to be put off that we were all coming. Her loss."

"Sorry," I said. "I guess you'll have to settle for us."

"That's okay." Stormy smiled. "It's a shame she feels that way. It's really too bad. You are my friend as much as she is."

I am? I wanted to say. It was so sweet of her to say and

so cool to hear. I had made it into Stormy's inner circle. "Thanks," I said.

Stormy seemed so mature. She headed off to one of the costume aisles.

"So, are you meeting up with Trevor?" I asked Scarlet.

"No, he wants to work the haunted house," she said, disappointed. "I'll have to see him afterward. But I told him he'll have to make up for lost time."

"You really like him, don't you?" I asked her.

"I do," she said.

I was happy for Scarlet that she found someone she liked. However, I wasn't so happy that it was Trevor. I still wasn't sure how much he cared for her, and I didn't want my friend to get hurt.

"What do you think of this?" Scarlet asked, holding up a cute devil outfit.

"It looks cool!" I said.

"I like it, too, but I'm thinking of going for something different. Out of my comfort zone." She buzzed off into another aisle.

"So who is your official date for Halloween?" I asked Onyx as she eyed the costumes. "Sebastian or Jagger?"

"I'm thinking of going solo," she said. "Jagger will be busy that night with his operations. And there will be tons of girls there. Sebastian will have his hands full—he is a flirt, you know."

"Not since he's set his sights on you. Other than

dancing with Stormy, he seems fixated on you," I said with a wink.

"You think?" she asked.

"I know."

Becky modeled a pink-and-purple butterfly costume. "I think it's adorable," she squealed.

"I think you should wear this," I said to Onyx as I held up a Cleopatra wig and costume. "It seems fitting. Marc Antony or Julius Caesar?"

"Yes," she said. "I love it!"

"I can't find a thing," Stormy said as she tore through the costumes.

"I think I found what I want to wear!" I pulled it over to find Scarlet holding the same outfit. It was a preppy school uniform.

"I wanted to embrace the lighter side," she said. "And I thought Trevor would love it," she said. "I guess you had the same idea?"

"Not the Trevor part," I said. "But I usually go preppy on Halloween. Last year I was a tennis player."

"Really?" she asked, surprised. "I bet no one in town recognized you."

"It's fun to dress up differently for the night," I said.

"Why don't you wear it?" she suggested. "I'm sure Alexander is dying to see you all prepped up."

"Are you sure?"

"Yes," she said, spotting another costume. She held up a red-and-white soccer uniform. "This one is perfect for me. I'll have Trevor really drooling."

I examined my preppy uniform. Though it wasn't me, it really was quite pretty. I couldn't wait to get all decked out.

"I can't find anything!" Stormy's temper began to flare.

"It's okay," I said. "There are tons of costumes here. We're bound to find you one."

She tore back into the aisles. "I found it," she said, holding up a Princess Leia outfit. "I know Billy and Henry will love it!"

"Yes," I said. "It will be their dream come true!"

12

Haunted Happenings

It had been a year since I'd trick-or-treated at the Mansion, Trevor had tried to graffiti the outside walls, and I had seen a dark figure standing in the attic window. And a year later, I was dating that mysterious shadow—a handsome vampire—and he was taking me to the Haunted Happening at the Crypt.

I waited for Alexander and Stormy at my house. I was dolled up in a short plaid pleated skirt, white socks and loafers, and a white Oxford. I topped it off with a blue headband. I caught myself in the mirror and actually liked the way I looked. I found my brother and his nerdmate in the family room. Henry was a Jedi Knight and stared at me as if I were the girl of his dreams.

"Raven?" Billy asked, dressed as Luke Skywalker. "Is that you?"

"What do you think?" I asked.

"I think now you might actually have a chance of getting into college," he said.

The doorbell rang, and I was met by Stormy dressed as Princess Leia and Alexander dressed as Jack Sparrow. Alexander looked gorgeous in his swashbuckling outfit, and Stormy was the perfect *Star Wars* princess.

When Stormy entered the hallway, Billy Boy's and Henry's eyes almost popped out of their heads.

"I'm ready to go!" she exclaimed.

The boys grabbed their bags and headed out of the house.

Alexander and I watched as the threesome walked down the street. Stormy quickly waved good-bye to us as she slipped into the night with her friends. She didn't even bother looking back. The *Star Wars* gang laughed and talked as they headed up a neighbor's driveway and rang the bell, ready to load up on candy and a full evening of treats.

Alexander and I got in the Mercedes, and he drove extra cautiously as we passed several werewolves, ghosts, and witches.

This night was another dream come true for me. I'd been to our local radio station—sponsored haunted house when I was a little girl, but I hadn't been spooked by any of the adults trying to act ghoulish.

We met Matt, as Superman, and Becky, dressed in her butterfly outfit, at the gravel road by the abandoned factory. There was already a long line of screaming girls with guys trying to be their haunted-house heroes. I wasn't sure what was so scary, but I was excited to find out.

As we approached the club, the scene was as frightening as it could be. There were several bodies lying on the gravel road that led to the Crypt, and body parts poked out of the ground.

"Gross!" Becky said, freaking out. "I'm so scared."

"This is really cool!" I said. "Jagger spared no expense!"

There was no way to enter the Crypt without stepping over a few fallen bodies. This obviously was part of the plan. Would they awaken from the dead and grab our legs? It was so dark, it was hard to tell which ones were real and which were fake.

I held my breath and stepped over.

"It's all right," I said, trying to coax Becky. "They're just props."

My best friend was frozen with fear. She wasn't about to move—even to flee the gruesome scene.

"It's okay," I encouraged. "I did it. It's not real."

She closed her eyes and took a shaky step forward. When her foot landed, she opened her eyes and moved to bring her other foot to the doorway. As it made its way over the body, an arm crept up and grabbed her ankle.

She shrieked so loudly, I thought she'd have a heart attack. She tried to wrangle her foot away, and I couldn't help but laugh out loud. The zombie sat up and laughed a monstrous laugh and released her. She raced into Matt's arms. Then we all laughed hysterically—even Becky.

We walked up the rickety bloodstained stairs to the Haunted Happening. We gave a bouncer our tickets and headed inside.

We walked down a long hallway that resembled an ancient tomb.

"Have we gone the right way?" I asked when we hadn't seen any hauntings.

Then, all of a sudden, out of the darkness popped a dismembered head, which hung from a rope in front of us. Becky and I screamed. Even Matt was startled. It swung back and forth. When it began to speak, we screamed again.

"Welcome to the Haunted Happening," it said.

We turned the corner and discovered a monstrous school setting. The teachers were zombies, and the students were passed out.

The zombie teachers came out to the edge of the setting where a rope separated the attraction from the visitors. They leaned over and tried to grab us.

Becky hid behind me and Matt.

The next room was the Chainsaw Massacre. We could hear the sound of the chainsaw but only saw the bodies and a bloody girl who was strapped to a chair, begging for our help.

When the serial killer raced in with his chainsaw, Becky screamed and clung on to Matt.

But I waved the frightful guy over.

"Do you need a hug?" I asked.

He was very startled and taken aback by my question. Several Prada-bees yelled around us.

The deranged lunatic came over to me and gave me an awkward embrace. Becky shook while Matt and Alexander cracked up.

We went into the next area, which was dark except for a few glowing candles.

Just then I was grabbed around the waist.

"Alexander," I said, but then noticed Alexander was on the other side of Matt.

This time I screamed. I turned around. It was Trevor, dressed as Nosferatu.

Alexander and Matt laughed, but I continued to scream.

"Get off of me!"

"I've come to suck your blood!" he said with a ghoulish laugh.

"Help!" I cried. "Get him off."

When he came for my throat, no one seemed concerned.

"Alexander—Becky!"

It was evident to me that Trevor was about to kiss me. But I wasn't sure anyone else was aware of that.

Finally Alexander noticed. He pushed Trevor away from me and glared at him. "The actors aren't supposed to touch the patrons," he said, his fists clenched.

"I'm not an actor," Trevor said, and disappeared behind the scenes.

We made our way into the next room, which was pitch black. We held hands and reached out to find our way through the maze. Alexander wasn't any help, letting Becky, Matt, and me flounder in the darkness.

"Gross!" I said as I felt something soft on the walls.

"It feels like . . . people!" Becky screamed.

"I think it's brains," Matt said.

"I feel a door handle," I said.

"Open it and get me out of here!" Becky was almost crying.

I turned the handle and threw open the door. We found ourselves in the Crypt—just a few yards away from the main dance floor. Jagger was a genius. Everything he did was one hundred and ten percent spooky.

I spotted two goths by the dance floor and did a double take. I was surprised to realize they were Heather and Courtney, two of the Prada-bees.

"I like your 'costume,'" I said sincerely as I approached them.

"Yours, too," they said nicely.

"I love that skirt," I said, gesturing to Courtney's ripped indigo-colored mini.

"Yours is very pretty, too," she replied, referring to my pleated plaid one.

For a moment we pleasantly eyed each other's outfits, not knowing what else to say. We were still different people deep down inside, but for one night, we both got to see how the other half lived.

I caught up to my friends and we headed straight over to Romeo, who was coolly dressed as Frankenstein's monster, to get some drinks and refuel.

Matt, Becky, and I ordered sodas, but Alexander was particularly thirsty.

"I'd like a Dracula's Curse," he said to Romeo.

"That's not on the menu," Becky said.

"It is for some people," Jagger said from behind us.

"Would you like to try one?"

We turned around. Jagger was creepy in a skeleton costume. His white hair with blood-red tips flopped over his bony face.

"How do you like the Haunted Happening?" he asked.

"I love it!" I exclaimed.

Becky quaked in his presence as Romeo slid the blood-filled drink to Alexander.

She and Matt watched, stupefied, as Alexander drank the dark red drink.

As soon as my friends regained their composure, we headed over to the dance floor, where we found a soccer-uniform-clad Scarlet and Onyx as Cleopatra already bopping to the killer music, along with Sebastian, who was dressed as a cowboy in a ten-gallon hat and cowboy boots.

"Having fun?" I asked.

"Yes—just us girls," Scarlet shouted. "Trevor is working the crowd in his costume."

"Yes, I bumped into him," I said.

"And Jagger is overseeing everything," she continued.

"Where's Stormy?" Scarlet asked, hot and sweaty from dancing.

"She's out trick-or-treating with Billy."

"Well, there is someone here who wants to see her," Scarlet said as if it was a warning.

"Who?" Alexander asked.

Just then pink hair popped out from the crowd. Luna was fabulously amazing as the Bride of Frankenstein with a pink monster-do. And following close behind was a familiar boy with white hair, dressed as Beetlejuice. It was Valentine Maxwell—the Maxwell twins' younger vampire sibling.

"Where's Stormy?" Luna asked, pulling at her long white gown.

"Trick-or-treating with Billy."

"Who's Billy?" Luna asked.

"He's my brother," I said emphatically.

"Well, we thought she'd be with you," she said in a huff. "Valentine would love to see her."

"Hey, Valentine," Alexander said. "I haven't seen you in a while."

"Hi, Alexander." Valentine smiled, his green eyes shining brightly. "Do you like my brother's club?"

"Yes, it's awesome," Alexander raved. "And so was the haunted house. It seems to be doing pretty well, too. I didn't know you were coming to town."

"I came in for Halloween. I was hoping I could see Stormy—and Billy and Henry."

"They aren't coming here tonight. They are out trick-or-treating," Alexander said.

Valentine's disappointment was palpable. "They are all hanging out together?"

"We didn't know you'd be here," Alexander said. "Otherwise—"

"I know. But Stormy loves Beetlejuice. I wore it for her."

I felt sorry for the youngest Maxwell. He was bummed out not to be among his peers. I couldn't blame him, but I wasn't so sure that I wanted him hanging out with my brother. Last time Valentine met Billy, he took him to a cave where he tried to bite him. I wasn't so sure my brother should be in his company again. In fact, I knew it wasn't a good idea.

"He's been really busy," I said. "Tons of science fairs coming up."

"Well, we'll still have to get together soon. And at least I'll get to see Stormy now that she's in town, too," he said. "We can hang out here at the Crypt."

"Yes, we'll see what we have planned," Alexander said. He didn't seem so eager for his sibling to be hanging around the younger Maxwell, either.

When Alexander and I arrived at my house, we found the sugared-up space invaders in the family room watching *Friday the 13th*.

"You'll never guess who we saw tonight," I said.

"Frankenstein?" Stormy asked.

"No."

"Freddy Krueger?" Henry asked.

"No, Valentine Maxwell," I replied.

"Who would dress up as *him*?" Billy asked.

"No one," I said. "He was at the Crypt."

"Valentine?" Billy and Stormy said in unison.

"He's here?" Henry asked.

"Yes," I replied. "He came in for Halloween."

"When can we see him?" Stormy asked.

"We'll have to go to the Crypt tomorrow," Billy insisted.

There was one person I didn't want to go to the Crypt and that was my little brother. Not only didn't I want the responsibility of bringing him to a club filled with young adults, many of whom were vampires, but the Crypt was my place, not his, and I was territorial over it. "We'll see. Besides, it's getting late," I said.

"Here, Raven, I saved these for you," Stormy said, handing me spooky spider tattoos.

"I love these! Thanks so much, Stormy," I said.

"And I'm saving this for Luna," she said. She held out a pink plastic skeleton ring.

"I'm sure she'll love it," I said sincerely.

"I had a blast," Stormy said.

"How was the haunted house?" Billy asked.

"It was really cool," I said. "You would have loved it."

"Well, it's getting late," Alexander said. "We really should be getting home."

"But we just got back!" Stormy whined. "We were just going to watch *Halloween*!"

"It's okay," Billy said. "You guys can watch, too."

Stormy looked at Alexander with puppy-dog eyes.

"I love *Halloween*, too," I said. "Can we all just watch?" I nuzzled up to my swashbuckler.

"Sure," Alexander said. "How can I say no to such pretty girls?"

"Thanks, Alexander," Stormy said, and hopped on the couch with Billy and Henry.

I scooted close to Alexander on the loveseat. "I'm going to be scared," I said. "You'll have to protect me."

"I'll do my best."

We dimmed the lights and pigged out on candy as Michael Myers hunted Laurie Strode.

After the movie was over, Stormy grabbed her candy and she and Alexander headed for the front door.

"I had the best time ever!" Stormy squealed to Billy and Henry.

"We'll have to hang out again soon. I have tons of scary movies to show you," Billy said.

"I do, too," Henry chimed in.

"I can't wait!" she said.

I was pleased that Stormy had had such a good time with my brother.

When it came to them saying good-bye, there was an awkward pause between Stormy and the two other trick-or-treaters. She extended her hand to Henry. He looked at her formality oddly but reached out to accept her hand. When he did, she instead reached in and hugged him. By Henry's reaction, I'm not sure if he'd ever been hugged by a girl before. It was too cute for words.

Then she leaned in and hugged my brother. They held on for a little bit too long, until Alexander cleared his throat and said, "It's time to go."

I walked Alexander to his car, and he gave me a long good-bye kiss.

I really liked Stormy being in town. As much as I didn't want to hang out with my brother, it was bringing out a sweet side to him, and I was impressed at how much of a gentleman he was becoming. And most important, Alexander seemed so happy having a family member at the Mansion. One who couldn't boss him around, even if she tried.

A few days later, Alexander thought it would be a good idea to let Stormy spend time again with her friends. She was so excited at the prospect of being with Valentine, Billy, and Henry that she was glowing. Alexander thought it would be okay for them to all be together, but I wasn't convinced that this particular mixture wouldn't be too dicey.

We dropped Stormy and Billy off at Henry's and headed back to the Mansion. It was too risky to have them hang out at the Mansion, with coffin beds in the Sterlings' rooms and a cellar full of blood, and my house was so small it felt like neither group would have any room to breathe. Alexander thought it would be safe for them all since Henry's parents were home. I wasn't sure what I was afraid of exactly. Billy getting bitten by Valentine? Stormy screaming about mirrors? I feared Alexander and I were being like her parents and not letting her spread her bat wings among mortals. It was time to give Stormy a chance again to develop friendships with her peers and truly have some fun.

Alexander and I returned to the Mansion for a little private time. I walked into his attic room and spotted a new painting he was working on displayed on his easel. It was smaller than many of his portraits that I'd seen before. This was an eight by ten.

I examined it closely. "That looks like Billy and Stormy!" Our siblings were dressed as they were the night of the dance.

"I thought since his picture wasn't going to turn out," my boyfriend said, "that I could paint him one."

"That is so thoughtful of you," I remarked sweetly. "I know he'll love it. Normally I wouldn't want a picture of my brother, but this time I think I want one, too."

"Well, this is for him," he said protectively. "By the way, has he mentioned that Stormy wasn't in the photo?"

"No, come to think of it, he hasn't," I recalled. "Maybe he hasn't checked yet or maybe we're off the hook."

"What are you going to say if he brings it up?" Alexander was seriously concerned.

"I guess the same thing I said to Becky about Sebastian not showing up in her pictures," I said, referring to the time Becky snapped a few of Alexander's best friend at a soccer game. "That she must have moved when it was taken."

"Will you be able to find a frame for this painting?" he asked. "You're good at shopping for those things."

"An excuse to shop? I'm your girl!"

Alexander kissed me long. But the picture of Billy and Stormy was staring at me. It was hard for me to concentrate when my brother was looking over my shoulder.

"You seem distracted," he said.

"I don't know if it's such a good idea to leave them alone. Do you?"

"How much trouble can they get in at Henry's?" Alexander asked.

Just then I heard my text beeping.

I let go of our embrace and grabbed my phone. It was from Billy.

STORMY FREAKED OUT. HENRY DARED HER TO EAT A CLOVE OF GARLIC. SHE'S LOCKED IN HENRY'S ROOM.

"Oh no!" I said.

"What is it?" Alexander asked, concerned.

I showed him Billy's text.

"I hope she's okay," I said.

"We have to get there now!" Alexander was alarmed. "Call Billy. I'll get the antidote."

I called and texted my brother but it went right to voice mail.

"He's not picking up!" I shouted.

Alexander stuck the antidote into a plastic bag and we raced down the stairs past Jameson, who was coming out from the kitchen.

"Where are you off to in such a hurry?" he asked.

Alexander didn't even answer his butler and instead rushed out the front door and into the Mercedes. I did my best to keep up with him, but I was huffing and puffing. This time Alexander didn't stop to open the door for me. He had one thing on his mind, and that was the safety of his sister.

Alexander peeled out of the driveway and raced toward Henry's house.

I kept calling Billy, but he didn't answer.

"Should we call the doctor?" I asked.

"I think we'll get there before he does," Alexander said.

Alexander pulled the Mercedes into Henry's long driveway. We hopped out. Alexander didn't even pause to shut his driver's side door. He raced up to the house and rang the bell relentlessly.

Henry opened the door, surprised to see us.

"Where is she?" Alexander demanded.

"Stormy?" Henry was still bewildered by our sudden presence at his house.

"Yes!"

"Uh . . . upstairs in my room."

Alexander took off up the stairs, and I followed close behind.

"Stormy?" Alexander called.

We passed several normal-looking bedrooms and a bathroom. At the end of the hallway was a movie poster of *Lord of the Rings* hanging on the door.

"That must be it," Alexander said.

Alexander pushed open the now-unlocked door.

We were both afraid of what we might find. Stormy was lying on the bed, pale and still. Valentine was holding her wrist as if he were looking for a pulse. Billy was standing next to them both.

Alexander rushed to his sister's side. "Are you okay?" Alexander shouted.

Stormy sat up. "What are you doing here?"

Alexander had the antidote in his hand.

"Can you breathe?" he asked her, himself breathless.

"Of course I can breathe!" She looked at her brother, bewildered.

"Did you eat garlic?" Alexander asked firmly.

"Uh . . . no," she said, confused.

"Did it touch you?"

"No."

"Did it come close to you?"

"No, I didn't even see any garlic," she answered, now frustrated.

"How about you?" my boyfriend asked Valentine.

"I'm fine," Valentine said.

"What are you talking about?" Stormy finally asked her brother.

"Billy said you ate garlic," Alexander told her.

"No—" she said. "And that was ages ago."

"What's that?" Billy asked, seeing Alexander's syringe in a plastic bag.

"Then what are you doing?" Alexander asked Stormy.

"Valentine's reading my blood," Stormy answered brightly. This was a power the youngest Maxwell possessed. By pressing on someone's vein, he was able to read their soul and innermost thoughts and feelings.

"I'm next," Billy offered.

"Billy sent us a text," Alexander said. "I thought you were eating garlic."

"I told you I didn't. We were playing a game," Stormy said.

"We were playing truth or dare," Billy said. "And Henry dared Stormy to eat a clove of garlic. Then she freaked out and ran up here."

"Don't you know you are supposed to take the 'truth' and not the 'dare'?" I asked Stormy.

"She locked herself inside until we promised we weren't going to make her," he continued.

"So what's so wrong?" Henry asked. "She dared me to eat a jalapeño. My eyes are still tearing."

Stormy grinned mischievously.

"Stormy is allergic to garlic," I said.

"I knew Alexander was," Billy said. "But Stormy, too?" They nodded.

"I didn't know that," Henry said apologetically.

"I know," Alexander said. "She could have just told you without freaking out."

"And so is Valentine?" Henry said.

"Yes," Alexander answered.

"That's odd. They aren't even related."

I breathed a huge sigh of relief.

"You didn't have to come over," Stormy said, embarrassed. "I handled this myself."

"Why didn't you answer your phone?" I yelled at my brother.

"It was on vibrate. I didn't hear it. It's downstairs."

I stared at him with daggers. "You are grounded."

"You can't ground me!"

"I can try," I said. "Where are your parents?" I asked Henry.

"They went out for dinner."

"Well, I think the party is over," Alexander said. "You should get off Henry's bed now." He was glaring at Stormy.

"I don't want to go!" she said defiantly. "We were just having fun. Valentine was reading my blood."

"Well, he can read it another time."

"I don't want to leave." Stormy stayed on the bed. "I want to find out what my reading is. Then Billy's and Henry's."

"I'll tell you what your reading is," Alexander announced. "And it's not pretty."

"I'm not going," she said stubbornly. "It isn't sunrise for another eight hours."

"Shall I have Jameson come and get you?" Alexander asked. "Or I can pick you up in front of everyone and carry you down to the car."

"You aren't the boss of me!" she declared angrily. "You spoil everything."

She hopped off the bed and stormed out of the room.

Alexander shook his head. "I knew she'd be a handful."

Valentine caught up to her in the hallway, and I overheard them talking.

"You like Billy—" Valentine said.

"What?" she asked.

"I read it in your blood. You like Billy. I thought you liked *me*."

"Stormy likes you," Henry said to my brother.

"Who told you that?" Billy asked.

"I heard Valentine," Henry answered. Then Henry whispered to me, "I was hoping she'd like me."

"I thought we were friends," Valentine said to Stormy.

Then we peeked our heads out of Henry's room.

"We are," she said. "But I have lots of friends now." She was as proud as she was sincere.

Valentine crossed his arms as Stormy headed down the staircase and out to the car.

"I don't understand a girl who doesn't like mirrors and is allergic to garlic," I heard Henry say to Billy. "I think I'm glad she likes you and not me."

alentine left, and after we dropped Billy off at home, Alexander drove me and Stormy back to the Mansion. When we got inside, Alexander talked privately to Stormy in her room while I waited in the library. When they were finished, he went to get a drink and I found her hanging out on her chaise longue, cuddling Phantom. She wasn't smiling.

"What's wrong?" I asked.

"Alexander doesn't want me to see your brother or Henry anymore."

"Well, I'll talk to him."

"I keep letting Alexander down. I hate disappointing him."

"Me too. I think he brings that out in people."

"He'll want to send me home if someone finds out about us. The garlic, the mirrors. Bringing blood to Hatsy's Diner."

"I don't think he'll want you to go home so soon. Are you homesick?" I asked.

"No," she said. "Just the opposite. I want to stay here forever."

"I want you to stay, too," I said sincerely.

"You'd like that?"

"Yes."

"But I thought I was getting in the way of you and Alexander."

"No, I like doing stuff with all of us."

"You are just saying that."

"I am not, silly."

"But I know he's really frustrated with me. We came so close to Billy and Henry finding out about Valentine and me. That's why he wants me to stay away from them and only hang out with Valentine—because I can be myself with him."

"That's not right," I said. "Besides, I don't think my brother thinks you are a vampire," I reassured her.

"It's one of the reasons my parents keep me at home and only let me spend time with other vampires. Everyone's afraid I'll spill the family secrets."

"Well, that's no way to live."

"But if people find out about us, they will fear us and persecute us. Like they did when my grandmother moved here to this Mansion. And she was just a mortal married to a vampire. Not everyone understands," she said. "Why do you?"

"I don't know," I said. "I was just born that way."

"I guess I was, too."

"It would be hard for me not to tell the world if I were a vampire," I said.

"Really? That's how I feel!"

"Yes, I'd want to shout it from the rooftops."

"You would?" she asked. "I just want to be myself."

"I know that must be very difficult."

"I don't like to hide away in our Mansion. I want to live and breathe. I want to explore the world and have friends."

"But someone as cool as you must have a lot of friends."

"I only have vampire friends. And not too many of those. Luna was one of my friends. Even though she was older and even when she was mortal. She understood because her family members are all vampires."

"Then maybe you should see her here," I said. "I guess Alexander and I wanted to be with you so much we didn't give you enough time to spend with her."

"Really?" she asked. "You wanted to hang out with me?"

"Of course! I've had a blast."

She smiled sweetly.

"And I know my brother has had a great time, too," I confirmed. "You should have friends your own age."

"And Billy, he looks at me oddly sometimes. Like he's trying to figure me out."

"He's probably looking at you because he thinks you are pretty."

"He does? He said that?"

"Yes."

She sat up, excited. "What did he say?"

"That someone as pretty as you shouldn't be afraid of mirrors."

Her soft brown eyes widened. "That's the sweetest thing I ever heard!" She beamed. "I want to see Billy and Henry. I want to have friends that are mortals." She looked at me desperately.

"You will," I said. "I'll make sure of that."

"Really?" she said.

"Yes, I'll talk with Alexander."

She leaned in and wrapped her arms around my waist. She squeezed me so hard I could barely breathe. Then she laid her head on my lap. "I felt differently about you when I first met you. I didn't think I'd like you. I was mad that you weren't Luna. And I was mad that Alexander stayed here and didn't return home to our family. I blamed you."

"I know," I said, stroking her hair.

"Are you angry at me for that?"

"You'd have to do a lot more for me to be angry with you. Besides, I'd be mad if someone kept me away from Alexander, too."

"You really like him, don't you?"

I nodded my head.

Even though there were a few more hours to sunrise, her eyelids were fighting to stay open. The pain of the evening wore on her.

"I want you to be a vampire, like me," she said.

"I do, too," I said to her, but she had already drifted off to sleep.

* * *

I found Alexander in the TV room watching *Dark Shadows*.

"We can't keep Stormy away from Billy and Henry," I said to him.

"I think it's for the best. What else can I do? Send her home?"

"No, let her have fun. Let her spread her bat wings," I said lightly. "She really is starved for friends as much as she is for blood. You said that yourself."

"I know. But tonight, when I thought she'd eaten garlic . . . I'm still shaking."

I gave him a hug. "I know it's hard for you. You want to protect her from the mortal world. You want to protect me from the Underworld. And in the end, it will only make all of us unhappy."

"But what can I do?" he asked. "I can't watch her twenty-four seven. At least when she's with Valentine or even Luna, they know all the secrets. I don't have to worry about that."

"But there are things she's missing. She can't live in your parents' mansion in Romania forever. Someday, like you, she'll grow up and move. She has to adapt and she has to learn how. You can help her do that."

Alexander realized that he could be the one to be instrumental in his sister's growth. This time he hugged me. "You are really a great friend to me, besides being my hot girlfriend."

"I try," I said, kissing him long.

"So what are we going to do now?" he asked.

"I can think of a few things," I said with a coy grin, "but they don't involve siblings."

* * *

When Alexander drove me home, we saw Valentine skate-boarding down the street away from my house.

When I got inside, I found Billy in the family room.

"What was Valentine doing here?" I asked.

"I've got to talk to you," Billy said urgently.

"What's going on?"

"Valentine told me I had to stop hanging out with Stormy." I could hear the agitation in his voice.

"What? He came over to say that?"

"He asked if I knew about Stormy, and I asked what he meant. He asked if I knew anything unusual about her, and I said, 'Yes, she's afraid of mirrors.'"

"Then what did he say?"

"He seemed relieved at first. But then he got all threatening. He told me that Henry and I shouldn't hang out with her anymore."

"He's not your father or Stormy's."

"I know, that's what I told him."

"And what did he say?"

"That I'm not like her and by hanging out with her I could put her in danger." He laughed. "Me, dangerous?"

I laughed, too.

"Then he asked to read my blood."

I stopped laughing. "Did you let him?"

"No. I was angry at him. That's not right for him to come over here and boss me around. Besides, what business is it of his who she hangs out with?"

"Well, I'm glad you stood up for yourself."

"I think I know why he's acting like that."

"You do?" I asked skeptically.

"Yes. I think he's in love with Stormy, and he's threatened by me and Henry spending time with her. They were close friends in Romania, but now she has learned there is more to life than guys with black fingernails and white hair."

I couldn't help but crack a smile. "I think you are right," I said, nudging my little brother in the arm. "Well, there's one person you and Henry won't be hanging out with anymore," I said. "And he just skated down the street."

Mirror, Mirror, on the Wall

Alexander and I had done our best to keep Billy and Stormy apart—but I felt responsible that they should be together again since their last time together ended abruptly. A few evenings later, Alexander texted to say that he'd pick me and Billy up to get ice cream at Shirley's Bakery with him and Stormy. Billy came into my room while I was getting ready for our outing.

"Don't you knock?" I asked.

"Did you know the picture of me and Stormy didn't turn out?" he asked.

"No," I lied. "That sucks. Are you just now looking at it?"

"I noticed it that night, but I was looking at it again this afternoon. You can't even take a picture right!" Billy argued.

"Don't worry," I said. "Alexander has—"

"But it's weird," he interjected. "She should have been in the photo."

"I guess I moved."

"No, that's not it."

"Then I guess *she* moved."

I'd used this excuse before on Becky, but my brother wasn't buying it.

"No, she didn't," Billy protested. "Henry and I enlarged it on the school computer. If you had moved, you wouldn't have gotten me in, either, or you would have gotten more of her. If she moved, it would have been blurry."

"Then I don't know what happened," I finally said.

"I think you do."

"I have no idea what you mean. What are you saying?"

"She didn't show up. The only explanation is that she's invisible on film."

I laughed. "Are you crazy?"

"No," he said. "It's scientific fact."

"Well, I didn't want to show you this. I wanted Alexander to give this to you himself. But now you've spoiled it!" I pulled the portrait of Billy and Stormy out of my closet. "Here—" I said, handing him the painting.

"This is so cool!" he exclaimed, gazing at the picture as if it were really her. "It looks like what the picture would have looked like."

"Yes, isn't that awesome?" I asked proudly.

"How did Alexander know that I'd want this?"

"I don't know. He just made it."

"He had to have known that the picture wouldn't turn out."

"He did not. Don't go all crazy conspiracy theorist on me."

"She's allergic to garlic and is afraid of mirrors," he said like a young Sherlock Holmes. "It's no coincidence, is it?"

"No," I said. "It's on purpose. Her parents purposefully altered her genes and personality to make her that way."

"That's why she doesn't have many friends," he deduced. "That's why she lives in isolation in Romania. That's why Valentine said she was different. He knows about her."

"Knows what?"

"That she's a vamp—"

The doorbell suddenly rang. And just in the nick of time. I raced down the stairs, and Billy chased after me.

Alexander and Stormy were waiting outside.

"Billy is asking a lot of questions about Stormy," I whispered to Alexander as I took his hand and hurried to the car.

"Like what?"

Billy caught up to me. "Hey, Alexander, Stormy."

The Sterling siblings greeted my brother.

"Thanks for the portrait of me and Stormy," Billy said to Alexander. "That was awesome!"

"What portrait?" Stormy asked.

"Alexander made a picture of you and me at the dance.

The same one that Raven took of us. It didn't turn out, so I was really lucky you made this."

He pulled out his phone. "I'd like to take another picture of us," Billy said. "And this time I'd like Alexander to take it. I bet he'll do a better job than you."

We all froze. None of us knew what to do. Take the picture and have it not turn out again?

"We'll do that when we get home," I said, pushing my brother out the door. "We need to get to Shirley's before there's a line."

I tried to talk as much as I could on the way to Shirley's Bakery. I didn't want my brother bringing up to Stormy that she was missing from his photo.

"So are you and Valentine good friends?" Billy asked after we got to Shirley's and ordered. We were walking along the downtown square and taking in the evening air.

"Yes, I've known him most of my life."

"Do you hang out a lot?"

"I don't have many friends at home. So I'd say yes, he's one. But since I came to this town, I have even more friends," she said with a twinkle in her eyes.

"Maybe we could get together tomorrow," Billy said suddenly.

"Tomorrow?" she asked. "Maybe later . . . How about after sunset?"

"I was thinking before. We could hang outside. Henry has a tree house. It will be better to see it during the daylight hours."

"I think I have something planned with Alexander."

"Then how about the next afternoon?" he pressed.

"Don't you have school?" she asked.

"We could meet right afterward."

"I get tutored by Jameson."

"I could come and watch," he said.

"Don't you understand? I can't see you then. I want to, but I can't."

"Why not?" he urged.

"I have something planned every day!" she shouted.

"What's going on?" Alexander asked.

"Nothing." Stormy took a bite of her ice cream.

"I was just seeing if Stormy could hang out with me and Henry during the day," Billy said. "We always go out at night. I'd like us to hang out in the day sometime, instead."

"That's not possible," she said.

"Why?"

"Stormy will be going back to Romania soon," Alexander said flatly.

"I will?" Stormy said, surprised.

"She will?" Billy and I asked sadly, in unison.

"I'd like her to spend the days with me," Alexander said. "You know, to catch up before she leaves."

"I'm not ready to leave," she said.

"You can't stay here forever," Alexander replied.

"I want to stay here," she demanded, "with Billy and Henry and Valentine and Raven."

I felt touched that she felt the need to be with me.

"We can talk about this later," Alexander said softly.

"No, we can discuss this now. I'm not going home!"

Stormy was getting mad, and I wasn't sure what to say or do.

"Well, you have to sometime," Alexander said. "We'll talk about it when we get home."

"I don't have to leave now," she said. "And you can't make me."

Stormy hurried off and sat on a bench outside the bakery.

"I'm sorry—" Billy said to Alexander. "I shouldn't have brought all this up. We can hang out whenever it's convenient," he said. "Just as long as she can stay here."

My brother joined her, and the two sat on a park bench outside a coffee shop. I noticed Billy fiddling with something in his back pocket.

He pulled out the mirror he'd taken from Henry's telescope. I wasn't sure what he was going to do with it, but I had a pretty good idea.

"Don't you dare," I whispered to him.

"Why not?" he asked, faking naïveté.

"Because I said so." I sat down next to him.

Stormy was busy licking the dripping ice cream off her cone.

"What will I see?" he asked. "Or not see?"

"If you do this, I'll break your fingers," I threatened in his ear. "You'll never play a video game again."

"What's going on?" Stormy asked.

"Just sibling talk," I said.

"Oh, I know how that is."

"Maybe you should go stand by Alexander," I tried to prompt her.

"I like it here," she said.

"I just wanted to see your reaction," Billy said. "I wanted to see if you already knew. But I sensed that you did."

"Knew what?" I asked.

"Look up there," he said.

He motioned to a mirror hanging on the corner of the building. The kind of mirror that is used to help cars see the pedestrians before they came out of the alley. It was angled so that we could see the bench we were sitting on. I saw Billy and myself, but the seat next to Billy, where Stormy was now sitting, was empty.

My mouth dropped almost to the cement sidewalk below us.

My brother didn't say a word.

"I'm not leaving," we heard Stormy say. "My friends are here."

Billy gave me a knowing glance, then smiled sweetly at Stormy.

"I love this ice cream," she said. She held her cone out to Billy. "Want a bite?"

"A bite?" he asked, staring at me. "No, I don't think *I* do, but Raven? *She* might."

There was a lot of tension between Billy and me as Alexander drove us home. I didn't know if he'd say anything to Alexander and Stormy about his discovery or what he'd say if he did.

Hey, Stormy—why don't you show up in pictures or reflect in mirrors? I heard him say in my mind.

I kept the conversation moving, and I bantered on about mundane topics and recent movies I'd seen. Anything to keep my brother from talking about what he'd seen—or rather, *hadn't* seen.

When we arrived home, we were saying our good-byes when Billy spoke up.

"I want that picture, remember?" my brother said to me. "Especially if Stormy is leaving soon, I want a picture of us together."

"I'm not leaving soon," she said for us all to hear.

"It's late," I interjected. "They have to leave. Maybe next time."

But Billy had already placed his phone in Alexander's hand.

Stormy gladly stood next to Billy. It was as if she liked playing the part of the happy mortal.

Alexander looked at me as if I knew what to do. I turned away in frustration.

Alexander took the picture, then handed me the phone. I tried to hang on to it but Billy snatched it from me before I could delete the picture.

"Good night, Stormy," Billy said. "Good night, Alexander."

"Good night," they both said.

Billy went inside, and I knew if I stayed for a long good-night kiss, he'd have that picture already plastered on a social network site.

It was one thing to have Becky know the truth about Alexander and the other vampires' real identities—but quite another for my little brother to know. Could he keep a secret? I'm sure he had already told Henry by now. The two must have been concocting their experiments like young Einsteins.

I blew Alexander a kiss and ran inside.

In the family room, my mom was reading a magazine and my dad was watching college football. Billy was already upstairs in his room. I ran up the stairs and charged over to my brother and tried to grab his phone away from him.

"What are you going to do?" he asked. "Kill me?"

"That would be too easy."

"What are you two doing?" I heard my mom call from downstairs.

"So you admit it?" he questioned.

"I admit nothing."

"You saw what I just saw in the alley mirror," Billy said. "Or rather, what I *didn't* see. You can't explain that away."

"I don't know what you saw," I said. "You need glasses."

"I have twenty-twenty vision," he asserted.

Billy was fiddling with the phone, and I was ready to pounce.

"What reason could there be for not seeing Stormy in a mirror?" he asked.

"You are just plain crazy!" I shouted.

"Like a fox," he said. "I should have known."

"Don't you like Stormy?" I asked. "You think you are harassing me, but don't you see it is her who you are really hurting?"

For a moment Billy softened, until he saw the picture on his phone. Then his expression changed.

"It can't be. . . ." he said, his voice trailing off.

"See, I told you that you were a fool."

"This means she's not the only one," he deduced.

"What?"

"You don't have many pictures of Alexander, either."

I didn't want to admit anything to my brother—but I

didn't know what to do. I was running out of excuses.

"Why don't you have any pictures of Alexander—that aren't painted—or one that isn't computer generated?" Billy was fixated on me. "Why is Stormy afraid of mirrors?" he went on. "How come she didn't show up in the mirror outside Shirley's? I've never seen Stormy or Alexander in the daylight. And why are they all allergic to garlic?" he asked. "Even their parents were when they came over for dinner."

He showed me his phone. There was just a picture of him—and an empty space where Stormy should have been.

"It doesn't mean anything!" I said. "Alexander moved, Stormy moved. Blah blah blah," I defended. "It happens all the time."

"No one moved," Billy argued. "I have another one like it taken on the night of the dance printed out upstairs. That is why Alexander made me a portrait of me and Stormy. Because he knew I'd never have a photo of her."

"So your phone is messed up," I charged. "That explains it all."

Then Billy looked at me right down in my soul. He was gearing up to take me down with his words.

He took the phone and shoved it in front of me. "This is Henry's phone!" he proclaimed.

My heart plummeted. It was as if he was the detective in a whodunit novel and he was holding the stolen goods with my fingerprints on them.

I was speechless. And so was Billy. It was as if all the color had washed away from his cherry-red cheeks.

"You're dating a vampire," Billy said, his voice quavering.

I didn't know what to say. My brother looked to me for a response.

Just then my mom burst into his room. "What is going on?" she asked. "No hellos? Only screaming?"

"Uh . . ." I said.

"I was just showing Raven this picture of me and Stormy," he said.

"Oh, really? I'd love to see it."

I gave my brother a stern glare.

He looked to me. He knew that if he showed it to my mother, then he would be putting Stormy in jeopardy. I could see him contemplate if that was worth the joy of harassing me.

Billy turned to my mom. "It didn't turn out," he said, putting the phone on his desk.

"That's a shame," she said, disappointed. "I would have loved to see you two together."

"I would have, too," he mumbled under his breath.

"So, how was your evening?" she asked us.

"We had a blast," I said.

"And you, Billy?"

"Uh . . . yeah, it was interesting."

"Interesting?" she said. "I thought you went to get ice cream. What is interesting about ice cream?"

I waited for my little brother to blab the News of the

Underworld to my mom. I was ready to pounce on him when he did.

"They had a new flavor," he said to me. "Vampire bites."

"Well, I bet Raven loved that one," she said.

I nodded enthusiastically. I was biding my time, hoping my mother would leave so I could talk to Billy alone.

"Sounds like you both had a great time," she continued. "I think this has been really wonderful for you. The fall dance. Now hanging out together. I think the Sterlings have bonded with you both and brought you two together. It's so sweet."

We both smiled fake smiles, and my mom, happy with the children she dreamed for, left the room.

"So you admit it!" Billy Boy said to me when she was out of sight. He had obviously been waiting all night long to talk to me about this.

I didn't know what to say. All my excuses flew out of my head. I couldn't figure out anything anymore to explain the bizarre behavior of Alexander, Stormy, or their parents. I couldn't rationalize why they acted the way they did, and I wasn't sure I even wanted to anymore.

I didn't respond. Instead I started for my room but then turned around.

"Thanks for covering with Mom," I said. "I know you did it for Stormy. But it really helped me and Alexander, too."

"So . . . it's really true," he said as if it was just sinking in.

I headed over to him. "You can't tell a soul."

"You are dating a vampire. . . ."

"I mean it. No one can know."

"But don't you see? This is major news. The existence of vampires. Not just in folklore—but in reality."

I leaned in to him with serious conviction. "Your lips are sealed. Promise?"

"Can I tell Henry?"

"No!"

"But he has to know! We could win a lifetime achievement award at the school's science fair."

"I don't need fifty media trucks parked outside the Mansion waiting to interview Alexander or Stormy to find that they don't show up on camera. He'll have to leave town. And that is not going to happen!" I pinched his arm.

"Okay, okay," he said, and I released him. Then he started processing the information. "I went to a dance with a vampire," he said. "I'll be the coolest kid in school."

"I told you, you can't tell anyone!"

"But how will I be cool if no one knows?"

I remembered how Billy treated Stormy and danced with her in front of the entire school. And now, not blurting out the identity of my boyfriend to my mom. "I think you already are the coolest one there," I said truthfully.

He gazed up at me with little-brother eyes. It was as if they were the words he'd been waiting to hear from me all his life.

I turned to leave.

"Hey, Raven."

"What—"

"Does this mean that you'll . . . ?"

"What?"

"Does this mean that you'll become a vampire, too?"

I smiled at my brother and spoke to him honestly. "I can only hope!"

I gave him a wink and started for the door.

"That would totally rock!" I heard him say as I headed out of his room.

For the next few days, Billy continued to want to know all about the Sterlings, the Mansion, and their family lineage. For years, he had seen me as the outcast rebellious older sister, and now I was suddenly the coolest sister he could have imagined in the world.

"You have to swear not to speak a word of this," I said to him one day after school. Our parents were still at work, and he found this an opportune time to hound me while I was eating a snack in the kitchen.

"I just want to know more . . . about vampires," he pressed while I sat at the dinette table picking at some chips. "What will happen?"

"Nothing."

"Will Stormy bite me if I see her again?"

"Uh . . . no. But I may if you keep bugging me."

"Will Alexander bite you and turn you into a vampire?"

"I hope so."

"I'm serious."

"So am I."

"I know you want to be a vampire," my brother said, leaning in. "But *really* be one?" he asked. *"Really?"*

"Yes. What's it to you?"

"You wouldn't dare do it. Not for real."

I rolled my eyes and turned away. "Let me eat," I said.

"You would," he insisted. "You really would?"

I turned back. "Why not? It's what I've always wanted. Wouldn't you be a Jedi Knight if you could?"

He looked at me affirmatively.

"Listen, the way I dress and the things I like," I began, "that's me. I'm not going through some phase. This is who I am. Get used to it."

"So you will get turned?" he pressed, wide-eyed.

"I'm not sure it will happen, no. But it would be cool."

"My sister, the vampire," he said.

"Well, I wouldn't worry about it now," I said. "I don't think it's happening anytime soon."

"You mean Alexander won't turn you?"

This time I looked at him affirmatively, but not with glee.

I took his once-bony arm that was now getting more muscular. "This secret remains between us. Everything you know and everything I've told you. If you tell . . ."

"I know . . . I won't live to see the next sunrise."

He withdrew his arm, and I returned to my chips. He

left me in peace as he headed upstairs mulling over a world he'd only imagined existing in folklore, which was now his new reality.

A few nights later, Alexander took me and Stormy to the Crypt. We all danced until exhaustion set in. Luna asked to have a bop with Stormy, and Alexander headed to the bar for a drink while I headed to the restroom to freshen my makeup.

On the way, I was stopped by Jagger.

"Having a good time?" he asked.

"Of course. This place is amazing," I said truthfully. I couldn't imagine that I'd lived so long in Dullsville without such a great place to hang out at. No wonder I'd always been so miserable.

"Can I show you something?" he asked.

"What? Me?"

"You've always been so into the Coffin Club and now this club. I'd like to talk to you about something."

"Let me tell Alexander."

"It will only take a moment." He stared at me, his blue and green eyes glistening. My curiosity was piqued and, before I knew it, he had his arm linked in mine.

He unlocked the small door that opened to the Covenant—the private club below the Crypt. He lit a few candles and led me down a staircase.

"Here, sit down," he said, offering me a chair.

"I think I should go back upstairs. Alexander will wonder where I am."

"This will only take a second. Besides, is he your keeper? Or do you make the decisions about your own life?"

I wasn't sure what he was driving at, but I didn't like him implying that I was a doormat, either.

Jagger sat down next to me and scooted close. "I want a partner. And the perfect person is you."

I wasn't sure what Jagger meant. "Your partner in the club?" I asked. "I thought Sebastian was your partner. Besides, I don't have money to invest."

"You don't need money," he said cryptically.

"To be part owner?" I asked.

"Yes. I have the key, and I will give it to you. I want to have you as part of my team. I want you to help me run the Crypt. You understand vampires better than most vampires do, and the same goes for mortals. And your style is amazing. Your passion and fearlessness are qualities I haven't found before. I could use them—you—to help me."

His proposal was exciting to say the least. I felt like I was Charlie in the Chocolate Factory. The keys to the factory? The ruler of the Magic Kingdom? The Wizard in the Land of Oz?

"I can make decisions?" I asked.

"Yes."

"About the club?"

"Yes."

"And help with future decor?"

"That's what I want."

It sounded like a dream come true. "And I can come here anytime?"

"Yes, you'll have your own office."

An office? I marveled. Like my dad had in our home—and the one he had at work? I only had my bedroom underneath my parents' roof. An office at the factory meant I'd have a place of my own, in the coolest place in Dullsville.

"In fact, you can sleep here, too, if you want. I think you'd fit in very well."

His words were macabre music to my multipierced ears. I could only imagine how much fun it would be, sleeping in the Crypt. Hanging out all night with Scarlet and Onyx, being by their side. Maybe I could even have my own coffin bed. Jagger seemed to really get me—genuinely understand what I wanted out of life and feel that I was the one who could help him even further with the Crypt. He'd get my morbid mortal expertise, and I'd get a set of keys to the cryptic kingdom.

"So what do you think?" he asked.

"I'm so flattered! I'd love to be a partner!" I said. "For the whole Crypt?" I asked.

"Yes," he said. "And for everything else." He placed his hand on mine.

"I don't know what you mean," I said.

He flashed his fangs at me. "Listen, we both want things. And why not marry them together?"

"What?" I was shocked.

"That's right, I'm talking about us."

"Us?" I asked. "There is no 'us.'"

"That's what I'm talking about. There *should* be an us. Only it should have happened sooner."

"But I love Alexander." I couldn't believe what I was hearing. I never knew that Jagger felt that way about me, so I was surprised by his romantic suggestion.

"I know you think you do. But what are the Sterlings providing you with?" he asked. "Nothing."

"Alexander—"

He inched in closer. "The Maxwells can give you everything. Immortality. Living the life of a vampire."

He drew his hand across my chin and down my neck. It sent tingles along my spine. I wanted to bat it away, but we locked gazes and I felt dizzy.

"Just look into my eyes," he said seductively. His eyes were hypnotic—the green and blue mesmerizing to me. There was a tiny part of me that wanted what he was offering—but I also knew I didn't want it with him. I wasn't sure if I could break his gaze or if I was just under his spell.

"I want this—but with Alexander," I proclaimed with all my might.

"I think you want this life so badly that you want it with me, too. Don't you? Just a little bit?"

Jagger was sexy in a dangerous way. If I didn't know Alexander—had never met him—I might have liked Jagger. But loved him? How could I want to trade my mortal life for one with eternal trickery? He was hot, no doubt, and the things he was proposing were what I'd always wanted.

However, they didn't come with the one I truly wanted to spend eternity with—Alexander.

Just then the back door to the Covenant opened and Luna stepped in.

"You can have a best friend," she said, "and a handsome vampire mate. And the club of your dreams."

"I already have a best friend," I said weakly. I tried to break his gaze, but all of a sudden I was melting under his spell.

For a moment we were dancing. I was in Jagger's arms. And though I felt woozy, I knew this wasn't a dream I was going to wake up from. He smelled like fire crackling over wood, and I was even more taken in by his scent.

I closed my eyes at last, breaking our gaze. All at once I felt like myself again and opened them. He smiled mischievously, and before he could lock his gaze with mine again, I pushed him away. "I don't want to. Not with you."

"It won't take long," he said. "The covenant altar is just over there. And it will feel so good. I promise."

He hopped up on the stage, and I froze.

Jagger was waiting up by the altar. "I'd like you to join me," he said. "You realize this decision is up to you. The keys to the castle. The vampire life. And me—someone who understands you. And what you've always wanted."

"You don't understand me. If you did, then you'd know I only want Alexander. Not you."

"But he's not offering you what *you* want. I am. Doesn't that speak volumes to who really cares about you?"

"You don't want me. You just want to get back at him."

"I don't. He and I are at a truce. This is about something different. How I want to go forward with my life. And I know I found the perfect partner for me. So if he isn't going to jump on the chance to have his dream girl—then I'm going to try to have mine. I can't help it if it winds up being the same girl.

"Just think about it, Raven," he continued. "There's no rush. You'll have all you've ever wanted, I can tell. I saw it in you at the Coffin Club and here at the Crypt. You are one of us. I can help make that happen for you. All you have to do is join me."

He lifted a goblet and smiled. It wasn't a creepy smile, but more alluring and friendly. Jagger was offering all I had ever wanted—only it was the wrong guy offering it to me.

"Just think for a moment," he said. "This could all be yours."

I would have everything. The Crypt. Sleeping with the undead. Living life in the Underworld. And finally being a vampire, myself. But the most important thing I'd be missing was Alexander. And to be a vampire without him—to be someone else's eternal bride—would be like living someone else's life. Not mine.

"You don't love me," I said.

"But I like you—a *whole* lot." He licked his fangs. "All you need to do is make the step. I can help you." He came over to me and offered me his hand.

I didn't take it.

"I can run for the door," I said.

"I know, but you haven't, have you? Is that because

you really don't want to?"

I wasn't sure. I think I was so surprised by his offer that I hadn't thought about escaping.

"Sit," he said, helping me down on the edge of the stage.

Luna placed two goblets on the coffin, and Jagger took one. "Here," he said, coming over to me. "You are only a sip and one bite away."

Jagger held the goblet before me and flashed his fangs.

I only had one option. I rose.

"So you are ready?" he said. "You won't regret this. We will share everything together. You and me."

I slid my hand in my purse and pulled out the one item that could save me.

I held my tube of garlic powder like a sword. "I only have to open it," I said. Both of his eyes turned angry red. His fangs flashed again. He would have lunged at me but he knew he couldn't.

Just then the door burst open.

Alexander, Sebastian, and Stormy rushed to the edge of the stage.

"What is going on?" Alexander shouted.

I felt relieved by Alexander's presence. I knew he could help me get out of this situation.

He leaped to the altar and pushed Jagger away. "Get off of her!" he said.

"I was just—" Jagger started.

"You can't explain yourself!" Alexander said. "There is no reason for her to be up here with you!"

Scarlet, Trevor, Becky, and Matt rushed into the Covenant.

"What's going on?" Scarlet asked.

Alexander glared at Jagger. "It's a good thing you are immortal. Otherwise you wouldn't survive this moment."

Luna raced up to Stormy. "It is not what it looks like—"

"What are you doing to Raven?" Stormy asked. "Are you trying to force her to bond with Jagger? She's going out with Alexander, Luna! How could you?" Stormy rushed over to me. "Are you okay?" she asked.

I was so grateful to be in the company of Alexander and Stormy. They led me off the altar and to my awaiting friends. Trevor glared at me, then at Jagger as if he was trying to figure out what was going on.

"I think it's time we tear this thing down!" Sebastian declared.

"I thought *we* were going to be together," Onyx said to Jagger. He just cracked a fangy smile in return.

Jagger and Luna slipped out a hidden door at the back of the altar without answering.

Alexander had mortals and vampires alike drawn to him, while the Maxwells had them fleeing. It was a sharp contrast in the reactions the three vampires brought out in people.

I can't believe Luna would do that," Stormy said the following evening when I met her at the Mansion. She was in her room touching up her makeup, and Alexander was still getting ready to go out with me.

She was disillusioned in her friend. "I knew you couldn't trust Jagger," she continued. "But Luna. How could I have been so wrong about her?"

"Well, she was always good to you," I tried to assure her, standing next to her at her dresser. "It's just that she's not so good to others."

"But if she isn't good to you—then that is wrong."

"I think she feels she's doing the right thing." I wasn't sure why I was sticking up for Luna. Maybe it was only to comfort Stormy's feelings. "Anyway, they were offering me something I wanted," I said, "just with the wrong guy."

Stormy had the life I had dreamed of. A casket sat in the middle of the wall where normally a bed would be. I sat down on the edge of her chaise.

"What do you want?" she asked, sitting next to me.

"To become a vampire."

"You really want to be one?" Her expression brightened.

"Yes," I said. "I always have. But I want to with Alexander."

"You'd change for Alexander?" She was shocked.

"Yes. But that doesn't mean I wouldn't want to be with him regardless."

"But you would become a vampire? Willingly?" she asked, surprised.

"Yeah. I've wanted it all my life."

"Even before you met Alexander?"

"Yes, but I'd only want to be a vampire with him," I said emphatically.

She grabbed my hand. "I didn't know you wanted to be like us, too."

"Exactly like you. Cool, nice, and living amongst your own."

"Does Alexander know this?"

"Yes. I've told him a hundred times."

"Then what is my brother waiting for?"

"He wants it to be the right time. And for the right reason."

"But if that's want you want—and he does, too—then why is he being so stubborn?"

"He thinks I won't like it. And that I'll blame him. He feels too much pressure."

"I guess . . ."

"But I know I will be happy. In fact, getting to know you has really convinced me how much I'd like it."

"You mean that?"

"Yes. You are the most fabulous girl ever," I said, using her favorite compliment.

"Not as fabulous as you."

"Really?"

"Yes. If I were a mortal, I'd want to be like you."

We smiled at each other, and Stormy blushed a little bit.

"And if I were a vampire—"

"But you can be!" Stormy interrupted.

"I'm not so sure he's ready." I sighed.

"You must tell him. Now. You must make sure he knows how important it is to you. Then we can be one big happy family."

Just then Alexander entered the room. Stormy and I rose, and I headed over to him. "What's going on?" he asked, kissing me on the cheek.

"Girl talk," Stormy said.

"Aren't you supposed to be with Jameson getting tutored?" he asked.

"Yes," she said. "Remember what I said," she whispered to me, and winked before she hopped down the stairs.

"I see you two are getting along."

"Yes, we really see eye to eye," I said, beaming.

A few minutes later, Alexander and I were talking in

the gazebo in the backyard of the Mansion.

"I still can't believe Jagger had you up on the covenant altar," he said, shaking his head. "After all he and I have been through. To do that to you—and me."

"I know."

"I'm just glad we came in when we did—but it seems you were able to handle yourself."

"It was more of an offer—" I said. "But still it was wrong. I had to get out the garlic powder for him to know I was serious, too."

The offer was attractive, and though I didn't want to become a vampire with Jagger, I was flattered that someone wanted to change me. I knew Alexander did, but Jagger was offering it to me only last night. It was something I couldn't shake. If Jagger wanted it, thought about it, and tried to make it happen, did that mean Alexander would, too?

"But why would he think that you would do that with him?" he asked.

"He just thinks of himself," I said. "But I also think that somehow he understands me."

"What do you mean by that?" Alexander was taken aback.

"He can see that it's really what I want. What I've always wanted."

"You don't think I understand you?"

"Of course I do. But I guess he's more impulsive. Like Sebastian. That's what makes you so special—your thoughtfulness," I said.

"Well, when it's time for you to turn," he said reassuringly, "it will be by me."

The stars twinkled through the broken boards in the roof. The night was perfect, and Alexander was giving me the dreamiest kiss I could have imagined receiving.

He slid his fangs down the side of my neck. As usual I was dying for him to take the plunge. When he pulled away, I followed him.

"I know your parents, your best friend, and now your sister," I began. "Unless you are hiding a brother and a dog, I think I've met your whole family."

"What do you mean?"

"Maybe now's the time. I see Stormy and how she lives. I want that life for me."

"You want to be isolated and in constant threat of being found out you are a vampire?"

"No. I want the other part. To sleep in a coffin by day and be awake all night. To live by candlelight. To be a part of the Underworld. I have craved these things all my life. I want to share that with you and your family and friends."

"But don't you already?"

"Luna has Romeo, and Becky has Matt. They are all sharing the same world. But us? We are trapped in our own separate human and vampire lives. Forced to live without being together as much as we could be if we were truly part of the same world."

"I know," he concurred. "I miss out on so much in your life, being stuck alone in my coffin while you're at school. I should be there eating lunch with you, studying, hanging out."

"That's how I feel about my life, too. If only I was a vampire, then I wouldn't be rotting away in school all day when I could be sharing a coffin with you, celebrating the night together, and be bonded together for eternity."

"I know I can never be a normal, mortal student. Maybe it's for the best, though. I'd be the dumbest guy in school. I wouldn't get any work done because all day I'd be staring at you."

It was sweet that Alexander wished he could live in my world. But I was dying to join his just as much as he longed for mine. "Well . . . I'm not sure it is for the best," I said.

"You're not?"

I faced Alexander straight on and stared into his chocolate eyes. "Even if you can't be a mortal, why couldn't I become a vampire?"

Alexander knew better than to answer.

I'd asked him a million times before, but tonight I was determined to know. I pressed further. "Don't you see? We could be together not only for eternity—but for every day."

When Alexander didn't respond, I continued. "Think of all that we are missing. Becky sees Matt every day at school and on the weekends." The more I thought about it, the more serious I became.

"I know. It's hard for me, too."

"It doesn't have to be anymore. This is something we can do for us. You and me. It doesn't matter what others will think. You said you didn't have the covenant ceremony with Luna because you were waiting to find the right someone. I thought I was that someone."

"You are. Don't ever think you aren't."

Even Stormy was convinced of that, I thought. All I had to do was to make my vampire boyfriend really understand how important this was for me.

"Then why not turn me?" I asked. I was more forceful than I had ever been with Alexander regarding this issue.

"It is hard for me, too, Raven. Since I first saw you. I told you, I crave you in a way you can't even imagine."

"Then let me finally fulfill that need."

"But don't you think you're too young to make such a life-changing decision? It's not only a life decision but an eternal one as well."

"Of course I'm not too young. I'm seventeen. I'm almost old enough to vote or join the military. Is there an age minimum on making decisions?"

"But you have to really consider everything. What if you don't like being a vampire?" he asked as if he was plagued with this concern.

"What's there not to like?" I asked. I knew he and I had often discussed whether the lifestyle I craved was the lifestyle I'd ultimately be happy with. But I knew I would.

"What if you hate it and then blame me?" he asked.

"Is that what this is about? That I will regret being bitten?"

"No . . . and yes. It's both. You would be giving up everything. It's so much pressure."

"For you or me?"

"For us both."

"But don't you see you've been the one changing all

along? You've stayed here in Dullsville when you could have returned home to Romania. You've left yourself in isolation without friends or family and only Jameson to keep you company. Now it's my turn to change."

"But people have different opinions as they grow. You might like vampires now, but what if you don't like them in the future and you're stuck being one for eternity?"

"I've been the same person since I was born. You know me, and I know myself. I don't follow trends. Believe me, my life would have been so much easier if I had been willing to do that. I could have been popular, maybe, not the outcast that I am," I said, reflecting. "Who knows? The one thing I know is that ever since I can remember, I've wanted to be a vampire. And I still do. And I've always wanted to be in love—and when I saw you, I knew that no matter what or who you were, I had to be with you forever. I may be impulsive, but I'm not fickle. I'll be seventy and still be wearing miniskirts and combat boots and wanting to be a vampire."

Alexander laughed, but I was serious.

"I need to know," I asked, looking him right in the eyes. "Are we on the same path?"

I was as surprised as he was by my forcefulness. But I remembered my and Becky's conversation about our futures. We'd have to be thinking of college soon and what we wanted to pursue for our futures. Did Alexander want the same things I did? Did he want me to share those things with him?

I was as excited about his impending answer as I was

afraid of it. If he wavered or was unsure, how would that make me feel? He'd taken my blood as his own, but would he ultimately go further? Would I be able to really become a vampire, or would we just continue to share our different worlds together?

"I need to know," I said again. Jagger's offer was flattering but not something I'd really consider since I loved Alexander. And now that Stormy wanted me to be part of the Underworld, I realized the only one who was reticent about my being turned was my one true love.

"What do you mean?"

"I want to know how you feel about our future."

"I thought you knew," he said with a sad expression.

I did know Alexander wanted us to be together, but I wanted to make sure he also wanted me to be a vampire—his vampire. I felt my blood boil. I wanted to be a vampire so badly that I needed the reassurance that I would be one day. "I just want you to tell me . . . that it will happen!"

"You want me to bite you now—or else?" he pressed.

"No, it isn't really an ultimatum. But how long am I supposed to wait?" I blurted out.

If I was turned when I was thirty, wouldn't that be good enough? I wondered. But even that seemed like light-years away from now.

He held my hand up, accentuating my finger where I wore his glistening eternity ring. "Doesn't this mean anything to you? Don't my actions speak loud enough?"

Alexander was taken aback. He released my hand and slid away from me. "Is that what this is all about, Raven?

You *waiting* to become a vampire? Not about us being together as ourselves?"

"No . . ." My heart sank. I had gone too far. I didn't mean to offend Alexander. He had given me a gift that every day reminded me of his feelings toward me. I was foolish to have pressed him. My need to be more like him—to be what I'd always wanted to be—had gotten in the way of our wonderful evening together. Why couldn't I just stay in the moment and let him enjoy having his sister in town and our privacy together instead of me demanding to be turned? Maybe I already was a vampire in a mortal's body. I craved Alexander so much I couldn't bear the thought of us not spending eternity together.

"I've waited seventeen years to meet you," he said. "The blood that runs through me isn't like yours. It is centuries old. You can live without me, Raven. I can't without you. You always act as if this is torture for you. But it's also torture for me."

I was struck by his strong reaction. I thought he was in a playful mood and would have just shrugged off my habitual pushiness.

"It's getting late," he said, rising.

Why did I have to know this minute? Didn't I have all that I wanted here in Dullsville without spoiling it? I had my whole life ahead of me—but I wanted everything now. I knew I was lucky enough to have Alexander and to have the Crypt, too. But there was always that piece of me that wanted to be a vampire just like I had since I was a child. But what I was asking Alexander to do wasn't something to be taken lightly. And I was letting my needs and impatience get the best of both of us.

"We should go," he said. "I'll take you home."

Just like Stormy had felt the night before, I wasn't ready for our evening to be cut short.

"No," I said. "Let's stay here."

"I have to check on Stormy."

"But I can stay here while you do that. Or I can come with you."

Alexander wouldn't be swayed and wasn't giving in to me, just like he hadn't given in to his sister. He was ready for the evening to end. He began walking toward the front of the Mansion.

It broke my heart to see him mad at me. We rarely fought. I thought I'd rather not become a vampire than have him angry with me. I didn't want to lose him altogether.

"Wait, Alexander. . . ."

He headed for the Mercedes parked out front, and I had to run to catch up to his quick pace.

He opened the car door for me but didn't wait until I got in before he went to the driver's side.

"I didn't mean to make you mad," I said, scooting in and closing the door.

"I'm not mad," he said. But clearly he was.

He turned on the engine and headed down the driveway.

I placed my hand on his shoulder, but he didn't cave in. His mood was like a jagged icicle thrust through my heart.

"You know how I feel about you," I said. "I just want to be like you, that's all. I should be able to tell you."

Alexander didn't handle his feelings like Becky and I did. Our every thought and mood flowed like Niagara Falls from our lips. Alexander kept his feelings to himself, and it pained me in ways that I couldn't express to see him shutting off from me.

I was angry with myself that I'd spoiled the evening, and with him, too, that he'd taken what I'd said the wrong way.

"I don't want to go home like this," I said when he pulled up in front of my house.

Alexander was too much of a gentleman to let me walk to the door alone. He came around and opened my door. When I didn't budge from my seat, he glared at me as if he would carry me out.

I exited the car and tried to hide the tear that began to trickle down my cheek as he headed for my door.

"You know I love you—even if I never become a vampire," I said to him when we reached the stoop.

His dark eyes softened as if he felt all the emotion behind my genuine words.

I was hoping for a good-night kiss or anything to show me that our misunderstanding was over. But he headed back down the drive instead.

I sat on the stoop. "I'm not going inside until you make up with me!" I called to him.

But this time my stubbornness didn't deter him.

He got into the Mercedes and drove down the street while my tears flowed.

I was devastated. What had just happened? Alexander and I were having the dreamiest night together, and I spoiled it by insisting again that he turn me. This time I'd pushed Alexander too far. He was more practical than I was, and that was one of the reasons I was so drawn to him.

I wanted to become a vampire. But I wanted it under the best of terms. Love, passion, and a visceral, physical, and spiritual need for each other. I didn't want to be matched up with someone like he'd been with Luna—or tricked like Sebastian almost was. And I didn't want the business transaction that Jagger had offered me. I wanted my becoming a vampire to have been thought through, carefully considered with both of our minds, hearts, and souls. If Alexander was impulsive and irrational like I was, then he would be a completely different guy—a different kind of person and vampire. And ultimately, that was not what I wanted. I thought about if I'd met Jagger instead of Alexander—who knows how I'd feel about being a vampire now? My life and eternity would be about tricks, menacing, and deceit. And if I'd been turned by Sebastian, it would have been about living eternity on a whim, not putting down roots but continually moving whenever he felt the need. We'd be slackers, running around from place to place without purpose. And though that seemed like it could be a lot of fun, I was more driven and motivated. I knew what I wanted out of life and out of eternity, and I wanted to share that with someone who knew what they wanted, too. Alexander had his passion in all the right places: his art, his family, me. And not only was he smoldering hot, he was just as attractive on the inside. He cared about me, his friends, and our families, and put our needs before his own. If not, wouldn't he be the kind of vampire who hunted girls and preyed on their flesh? Not the romantic, artistic type I found irresistible.

And asking someone to physically turn me into something that I wasn't born being wasn't to be taken lightly. If I'd been the one who had to turn Alexander into a mortal, become someone different from his own family, it would be a huge burden to me. I would do anything to make him happy, like he wanted to do for me, but I understood that it was a difficult decision to make. And if he'd felt any other way about turning me, with all its thrills and complications, then he wouldn't be my Alexander Sterling.

I realized that not having Alexander at all was far worse than my not becoming a vampire. If I had to live by his side just as I was, that was good enough for me. Any life with Alexander was better than a life without him.

T he next evening Becky found me in the family room, still in my pajamas, staring at a fiercely fanged and red-eyed Kiefer Sutherland on the TV with a box of tissues in my lap and clutching my eternity ring.

"She hasn't been out all day," my dad said to her. "She won't say what's wrong, but I have a feeling it has to do with Alexander."

"What happened?" Becky asked, sitting on the couch with me.

"Alexander hates me," I whimpered.

"He does not."

"We got into a fight."

"You two?" she asked, surprised. "I can't believe it. You never fight."

When I noticed my dad was out of the room, I leaned in to Becky.

"I wanted to see if he'd turn me—" I whispered. "And I pushed him too far."

"Did you make him bite you?" she asked, seriously scared.

"No. But I asked him when he would. And I pressed him too hard."

"Alexander doesn't seem the type to get mad."

"He does get angry—but mostly at the Maxwells. Not usually at me."

"Well, maybe he was having a bad day—or night," she corrected.

"I don't know. I get so impatient. Having Stormy here has been so cool. I see her life like what it would have been for me if I were born a vampire. And with every passing day, I feel like I'm missing out on being that person. Only when we had this fight, I realized . . . *this* is who I am. I am a mortal dating a vampire. And if that is all I ever am, then I am still truly blessed. I want Alexander more than I want to be a vampire."

"Does he know that?" she asked.

"Why wouldn't he?"

"He's only human . . ." Becky began. "I mean, I guess he's not."

We both laughed, though mine was through my pain.

"It has to be so hard to be a vampire," Becky continued. "Now that I know the truth about Alexander, it really got me thinking lately. To be goth is hard enough. But imagine being a vampire. It doesn't matter where you are—you can't really be yourself."

"That's what Alexander says."

"He should know," she said gently. "He's only protecting you, Raven. I would hope if Matt were in that position, he would want to protect me, too."

"Shouldn't Alexander be happy that I want to make the change with him?"

"I can't imagine asking Matt to change me into something I'm not. Anyway, out of all people, I thought you'd want to be yourself."

"But you know I've always wanted to be a vampire. Wouldn't you want to change into something you've always wanted to become?"

"Yes."

"I thought I could talk about this with him."

"Maybe when you are together, he doesn't want to talk," she said coyly. "Maybe he wants to turn you but wishes he didn't. And when you bring it up it only reminds him of the huge decision he will have to make someday."

"I don't want it if it's not with Alexander. Now I blew it. We can't break up." I wiped away a fresh round of tears. "I've lost everything!"

"It's okay," Becky tried to comfort me. "You aren't broken up."

"I don't know. He was really hurt."

"Let's go to his house. You can talk again, tell him how you feel. I'm sure this will all blow over in a heartbeat."

Becky helped me get myself together and handed me an outfit to wear. We got into her truck, and it felt like

an eternity before we pulled up to the Mansion. I imagined our conversation. I'd tell Alexander I was sorry, and
he'd refuse to see me anymore or agree that it was a big
mistake. I was hoping for the latter. Becky waited in her
truck while I jumped out, raced up the Mansion stairs,
and pounded on the serpent knocker. The ring Alexander
had given me shined in the streetlight. I'd been so foolish
to question him. He was a vampire and he needed me way
more than I gave him credit for, and, as usual, I had made
everything about myself. Now I was tortured, too, for my
foolishness.

Jameson finally came to the door.

"Is Alexander home?"

"No, Miss Raven, he went out a few minutes ago."

"Did he say where he was going?"

"No, but he did look like he was in a hurry."

"Who's there?" I heard Stormy ask.

"It's Miss Raven." He opened the door wide enough
for me to see Stormy at the bottom of the staircase. My
makeup and charcoal eyeliner couldn't hide that I'd been
crying.

"What's wrong?" Stormy asked. She pulled me inside.

"Oh, nothing." I tried to be strong. "Do you know
where Alexander is?"

"No. He was in his room all night and wouldn't talk.
Did something happen?"

"We got into a small fight."

She took me by the hand and led me into the parlor
room. "Sit down," she said like a lady.

I sat down feeling awful. I didn't have control over Alexander and how he felt about me—whether I'd really pushed him too far or he just needed time to cool off. The pain of our separation was killing me.

"What happened?" she asked.

I wasn't sure what to say to his sister. She could change her mind about me and tell Alexander how he was more meant for Luna than he was for me. But I'd gotten to know Stormy so well that I really thought we'd bonded. And I was so distraught, I needed to talk to someone, and there weren't many people in this town who I could talk to about the subject of vampire bites.

"I asked him about turning me," I said. "And I think I pushed him too far."

"You should be able to talk to him about anything."

"I thought so, too. But you know Alexander. He likes to be calm and rational. And I get impulsive, moody, and emotional."

"I do, too," she said.

She put her arm around me. "You have to know. It's because of you that Alexander didn't go back to Romania. It wasn't because he was mad at me because I told my parents where he was the night of the covenant ceremony. He stayed because he didn't want to leave you."

I was comforted by Stormy's kind words. "Thank you," I said. "But I think I blew it, though. I'm going to have him running home now."

"He's not like that. He gets angry and broods. He's a guy, after all."

"Where could he have gone?" I asked.

"Maybe Sebastian knows." She hopped off the chair. "We'll have to find out."

I gave Stormy a big hug. "Thank you," I said. "You really are a great friend."

She appeared truly pleased by my compliment and grabbed my hand as we headed down the staircase and out the front door.

Stormy got into Becky's truck with me, and we headed to Sebastian's apartment. I hadn't been to it before but I knew where it was.

Sebastian lived in a four-family unit in downtown Dullsville next to the Sugar and Spice restaurant.

The Mustang was there—but not the Mercedes. It wasn't a good sign.

I rang the bell a million times.

"Hey, dude, lay off the bell," we heard him say into the intercom.

"It's Raven. Is Alexander with you?"

"No."

"Can we come up?"

"We? Uh . . . Sure."

The three of us tromped up the steps to Sebastian's door.

"Hey, ladies. What's up?" Sebastian was standing in his jeans and with his hair damp as if he'd just showered.

"Have you seen Alexander?" I asked.

"No. What's up?"

"We were just looking for him," Stormy said. "Jameson

said he went out, but we don't know where."

"Are you okay?" he asked me. My eyes were still puffy; I felt like "crybaby" was written all over my face.

"Yes."

"They got in a fight," Stormy blurted out. "And when I find him I'm going to read him the riot act."

"You do that," Sebastian said with a chuckle.

"Maybe he went to the Crypt. I was supposed to meet him there later tonight."

I sighed. Maybe Alexander was there. I wasn't looking forward to trying to reconcile in front of all the vampires of Dullsville, but I didn't have a choice. I wanted to make up regardless of how or where it happened.

"Off to the Crypt," Stormy said.

"Hey, wait up for me," Sebastian said, putting on a T-shirt and boots. "I don't want to miss a thing."

Becky drove us to the Crypt, with Sebastian following closely behind.

When we arrived, I was anxious to find Alexander. We saw Onyx and Scarlet talking by the coffins.

"Is Alexander here?" Sebastian asked.

"We haven't seen him," Onyx said.

"We have to find him," Stormy explained. "It's very urgent."

"What's up?" Scarlet asked.

"I just need to read him the riot act," she said.

The girls laughed.

"He might be here somewhere," I suggested.

"I'm going to hang here, dudes," Sebastian said. He sidled up to Onyx, who appeared glad to see him. "I'll give you a buzz if he shows up."

Becky, Stormy, and I headed into the Crypt, where we ran into a younger clubster—Valentine. I wasn't sure if Stormy knew about Valentine and Billy's confrontation at our house. And I wasn't going to tell her about it now.

"Hey, Stormy!" Valentine said.

"Hi, Valentine. Have you seen Alexander?"

"No. Uh . . . did Billy come with you guys?" he asked.

"No," she said. "We came to find Alexander."

"Great! While you're waiting for him to show, we can hang out."

"Uh, I really need to find him," she said.

"You have all night. We can hang out together. Want a drink?"

"I'm not thirsty." She was distracted, scanning the crowd for her brother.

"Well, I am," he teased. "And it's not for anything served at the bar."

It was odd to see Valentine flirt with Stormy.

"I'll go and look for him and catch up to you in a few," Becky said.

"Thank you," I mouthed to her. I, too, was scanning the crowd for Alexander, and I wasn't about to leave Stormy by herself in the club.

"Why don't we dance?" Valentine asked Stormy.

"Maybe we can later," she answered.

Valentine appeared disappointed, but that didn't stop

him from trying other tactics. "Do you want to play pin-ball? My brother just got a cool machine in today."

"Not now," Stormy said. "We're on a mission."

"I'm glad it'll just be us hanging out from now on," he whispered to her.

"What do you mean?"

"Billy and Henry—" I overheard him say.

"What about them?"

"They're old news."

"What do you mean?"

"Ah, we don't really mix well together. After that night at Henry's. They could have really hurt us."

"But they didn't."

"Well, next time we might not be so lucky. Our kind needs to stick together."

"No, we don't. In fact, we need to branch out. And that's just what I am doing."

"Are you going to tell him what you really are?" he asked.

"No."

"What if he finds out?" he continued to whisper. "Raven knows. You think he wants to be one of us?"

"I don't know."

"Of course you do. And how do you think he'll respond to taking a vampire to a dance?"

"Is that what this is about? My going to the dance with Billy?"

Valentine did appear hurt when Stormy reiterated that she had gone with my brother to the fall dance. "When he finds out about you, how do you think he'll really respond, Stormy?"

"He won't find out!" Stormy said.

"You have to be friends with our kind," he insisted.

She looked at me. "Raven isn't a vampire," she said. "*And* she's dating one. Plus her friends are vampires. I want to be like Raven. I am a vampire and have mortal friends."

She shot me a triumphant smile; I was so pleased to know that Stormy admired me in any way.

"Besides," she said strongly to Valentine, "you can't tell me who I can or can't be friends with. And if that's the way you're going to be—then you aren't a true friend."

She grabbed my arm. "We have to go find Alexander," she said, and led me through a group of dancers.

Just then Stormy spotted Luna standing by the bar.

"I need to talk to her," she said, storming over. I followed close behind.

"Hi, Stormy Girl!" Luna squealed when she noticed the young Sterling. She opened her arms for a warm embrace but Stormy faced her with her hands on her hips.

"I thought you were my friend," she charged.

"I am." Luna was overly sincere.

"But why did Jagger lure Raven onto the altar?" Stormy argued.

Luna laughed as if the event were as mundane as getting pizza. "You know my brother."

Stormy wasn't softening. Instead she got angrier. "But you were there, too. Why didn't you stop him?"

"I don't know," she said. "It happened so fast."

"It did? It looked like it was something you both planned."

"Stormy," Luna said with an ultrasoft voice. "This wasn't about you."

"But it was. Alexander's my brother. And Raven? She is like my older sister."

Luna's blue eyes turned raging red. She quickly caught herself getting tense and tried to cover it up with a saccharine smile.

"Stormy," she began sweetly. "You don't understand. You're just a kid."

"I understand. Everyone says they don't trust you. And I have a sense of people not to trust. Jagger. Trevor. But you? I really missed the mark. You really let me down."

"I'm sorry, Stormy," she said as kind as she could. "I never meant to hurt you."

I really thought Luna was telling her the truth, as if she hadn't thought out the ramifications of her actions that night.

Jagger noticed us talking, and Stormy's stance gave off the appearance of a girls' feud. "What's the commotion?" he asked.

I stared him down.

"It's okay," he said to me. "The offer isn't good anymore."

When Jagger looked at Stormy, she wasn't budging, either. She stared up at the Maxwell twin with vehemence.

"Why did you do that to my family and friends?" Stormy charged. "Isn't it enough what you have here? This club? If it wasn't for Alexander, you wouldn't be here at all. You should be thanking him, not trying to stab him in the back."

Both siblings were shocked at her words.

Just then Valentine stepped out from behind us.

"So this is why you don't like me?" he said to Stormy. His voice couldn't hide his sadness but instead gave it away. "Because of them?"

"No—" she said to him, "it's not about them. I do like you. But I want to have more friends."

"It is their fault," he insisted. Now Valentine was the one squaring off at his older siblings. "You guys always have to make trouble. It's bad enough at home. But here, too? Why can't you leave well enough alone? Alexander likes Raven. Let them be."

"I was just trying to help Raven out," Jagger answered defensively.

"Well, you weren't," Stormy said. "If you want to help her out, just be her friend. And Alexander's."

I was so impressed with Stormy's arguments and sticking up for me in front of Jagger, I was speechless. But I'd let her take over for long enough, and it was time for me to step in.

"Having a dance club is nice, but not if no one here is your friend," I said to Jagger.

"I don't need friends," Jagger mumbled. But clearly he did. He liked being the popular one in town now that he owned the club. He gazed out at the crowd as if he was really wondering how many of them he could call his friends.

"It's funny," he said as if we weren't in the room. "I don't know these people. Even Onyx and Scarlet. They are all here because of the club." His voice was reflective and suddenly soft. "Alexander has been a friend to me. I guess I really never realized it until now."

Stormy relaxed her stance and appeared pleased with Jagger's reaction. And Luna was equally moved. She didn't want to be the only one who wasn't suddenly on the Sterling side.

"I'm sorry, Stormy," Luna said. "I really am. I didn't mean to hurt you, of all people."

I felt she seemed sincere. This time I think the example she was setting for her brother and her younger friend really hit her.

"Speaking of Alexander," Jagger said. "Where is he? I'd like to talk to him about that night."

"We were hoping he was here," I said. "You haven't seen him?"

They shook their heads.

"Were you supposed to meet him here?" Jagger asked.

"Uh, no. I just thought he might show up."

"Well, maybe we can dance until he does," Valentine said to Stormy.

"Uh . . . that would be great. But I really want to find him."

Valentine appeared deflated, and Stormy put her hand on his shoulder. "But the next dance is all yours," she said to her lifelong friend.

His sullen face brightened.

"If you see Alexander, tell him I need to speak with him," she said to the Maxwells. "Immediately."

They nodded affirmatively and gave her a smile.

We scanned every corner of the Crypt and finally saw Becky.

"I haven't seen him anywhere," my best friend finally said.

"Neither have we." I was disheartened. "Well, I guess we should go."

We left the club, and Becky drove us back to the Mansion to drop off Stormy.

"When Alexander gets home," Stormy said, "I'll give him a good talking to."

I leaned over and gave Stormy a big hug. She had become a really good friend to me, and I cherished her.

As we drove to my house, it began to pour. Becky dropped me off in the driveway.

"Thanks, Becky. I'll let you know if I hear anything."

"Don't worry, Raven. It will be okay. Someday you'll look back on this time and barely remember it."

"I hope so," I said, and dashed to the house.

There was one final place where I thought Alexander might be. I hoped I was right.

I hopped on my bike and tore down the road in the sprinkling rain. By the time I got to Dullsville's cemetery, it was pouring. I was drenched and my boots were soaked. But I didn't care. When I turned into the parking lot, I saw the sight I'd been longing to see—the Mercedes.

The cemetery was closed, and the gates were locked. Normally, climbing the fence wasn't too hard for me; I'd done it a million times. But tonight, the pounding rain made it hard to see and the wrought-iron posts were slippery. I grabbed them as tightly as I could but slid several times. With a few curse words and all my might, I wrapped my fingers and wedged my boots into the grooves and hoisted myself up.

I flipped myself over and lost my footing on the slick fence. I fell on my bottom on the wet grass with a thud. I swore some more and then laughed at myself. If I had only been patient, I wouldn't have been in this mess. Alexander and I would have been bopping at the Crypt, and I would have received romantic kisses, not solitude. Instead, I was on my backside in the mud in the graveyard, chasing after my angry boyfriend.

I got to my feet and didn't even bother trying to beautify myself. It was far too late for that.

I raced through the cemetery—past tombstones and memorials. And then I saw a figure standing in front of the Baroness Sterling's monument.

Even in the pouring rain and with his back to me, Alexander was a magnetic presence.

I knew he sensed me standing a few yards away.

"I'm sorry—" I called to him through the falling rain. "I didn't mean for us to fight."

He didn't respond or look at me.

"Alexander—" I said. "Please understand."

He slowly turned around. He was gorgeous, wearing skinny black jeans, monster boots, and a black T-shirt. He was soaking, like me, and even though he was angry, he was still as radiant as the handsome guy I'd fallen in love with. I wasn't sure if he was going to yell or walk away.

Instead, he just stared at me with his soft chocolate eyes.

I hurried over to him but didn't hug him. I wasn't sure if he was ready for me to.

"I never meant to hurt you—" I said. "I didn't want us to fight. I just wanted us to talk. It got out of hand. I never meant for us to get angry."

Alexander didn't respond but just listened.

"I looked for you everywhere—" I said. "At the Mansion, Sebastian's, the Crypt. I was ready to fly to Romania," I said, my voice breaking.

He still didn't respond but continued to let me talk.

Before our fight, I knew Alexander hadn't planned on leaving me, and I was immature to think he needed to sink his fangs in my flesh to prove that to me. I faced him strongly and sincerely. "I want to be a vampire," I said. "Your vampire—and if it is to happen, it needs to happen when we both are ready. If not, I am happy the way we are."

He listened to what I said but still didn't respond.

"Please say something—" I said.

He didn't yell at me or even kiss me. Instead he took my hand in his and gazed down at me and took a deep breath. His voice was deliberate. "Raven."

My heart fell. Was this the moment Alexander was officially going to break up with me? I had pushed him too far this time.

He gazed at me intently. "I've been thinking."

"About what?" I asked, worried. "Wait, Alexander, please don't say it—I came here to apologize."

"It's important for me to tell you this now," he said with a deliberate but urgent tone.

"No," I said. "I came here to make up, not break up."

He placed his finger over my black lips and shook his head. "Now it's my turn to speak."

I took a deep breath and squeezed his hand. I didn't want to let go under any circumstance.

"There is something I want to talk about." His voice was so serious, I was frightened. The rain broke, and the crescent moon shone brightly overhead. "You are so much like my grandmother. If she had been changed, then maybe her fate would have been different. I don't want to see you at covenant altars with other vampires. Only me."

He leaned in to me and gazed so intensely that I thought I could see his soul. "I want you to know I thought about it that first night I saw you outside my house on Halloween. And I've thought about it every night since then."

"Thought about what?" I asked.

"Turning you."

I melted. To hear it from his lips sent chills surging through me. I shouldn't have needed him to reassure me countless times. However, I did like hearing it. "You've told me you have thought about it, and I should have listened.

But I shouldn't have pushed you. I just want us to be like we were again. I don't want us to argue. I want us to be together. Like we discussed, I'll be turned when the time is right."

He took both of my hands. His rain-soaked hair was tousled and wild and his sexy dark eyes stared through me again. "I want you to know I think the time is right."

I was stunned. "What did you say?" I asked.

He leaned in even closer. "I think the time is right," he said with confidence. "For you to be turned. By me."

I was floored. I wasn't sure I was hearing him correctly. "Are you serious?" I had been waiting for him to call our relationship off and he was suggesting the opposite. I couldn't believe what I was hearing.

"Dead serious," he said with a heavenly smile. "I think the time is right for us to be together—forever. In fact, I know it is."

I didn't know how to respond. I was so taken aback, I was speechless.

He smiled a gorgeous smile. "You have waited for me," he said sincerely, "and I have waited for you. Now we need to stop waiting."

I was awestruck. I stared up at my vampire boyfriend. Was Alexander actually suggesting what I thought he was? What I'd wanted since I was little and even more so when I met him? Was this in fact the moment I had waited for all my life?

My hands began to shake and I felt as if I were in a movie. Time seemed to stand still. A vampire—the most gorgeous and mysterious one in all the world—was asking me to be his vampire mate for all of eternity. I was still at a loss for words.

"Have you changed your mind?" he asked, suddenly concerned.

"No!" I exclaimed. "I just can't believe this is really happening. Is this a dream?" I asked.

"If it is," he said with a sweet grin, "then I'm having the same dream."

I was overcome with delight.

"So what is your answer?" he asked. "I don't think I can wait forever for that. The suspense is killing me."

"Of course!" I burst out, and hugged him with all my might. "Yes! Yes! Yes!"

As we embraced, the pain of our fight escaped my body and the excitement of his proposal began running through it.

"I don't want you to be afraid," he said. "If you want to change your mind—at any point—I will understand."

"How could I be afraid?" I wondered.

"I'm a vampire, remember. And you'd be one as well."

The thought of my really becoming a vampire sent more chills through me. "I'm not afraid of you, or of becoming like you," I said. "Not now, nor will I ever be. This is what I've always wanted."

He smiled another gorgeous smile. We stared at each other, then he drew me in to him again and kissed me long. My knees were weak, but my heart raced and I was dizzy.

"Are we going to do it now?" I asked excitedly. I didn't

want to lose this moment by putting it off, but since I'd envisioned being turned by him so many times, I wasn't sure if I needed more preparation for the actual event. "I imagined wearing a pretty dress . . . not looking like a slug. But I can do it now if you want."

"We don't have to do it tonight," he said, guiding my dampened hair away from my face. "We can wait as long as you like."

"I don't want to wait too long," I said eagerly.

"This will change your life," he said. "You still have school."

"School? Schmool!"

"But that is just as important."

"I don't want to wait until I'm finished with school. That's more than a year away," I said impatiently. Then something important came to mind. There was one new person I'd want to see me change and she wasn't going to be in Dullsville much longer. "I'd really like to be turned while Stormy is still here. I'd like her to see me as a vampire. I want her to see me like I see her."

"She means that much to you?" he asked.

"You both do."

"But she's leaving next week."

"I know."

"But you still have classes, and your education is important."

"I can go to night classes. Or take online courses. Or even Jameson can teach me. I'll be homeschooled like you," I suggested. Now that Alexander was on board, I wasn't going to let anything get in our way.

"I thought—but what about your parents? Do you think they are going to be happy about this?"

"They won't understand at first. And they'll be angry. But I'll still be their daughter. I'll still live in Dullsville and graduate high school and go to college. And they were hippies. If anyone understands being different, it's them. I'll just have to remind them."

"We will have challenges," he said.

"I know. But if we are together, then we can take them on, together."

"I've never met anyone like you." He drew me in again and kissed me passionately.

Then we sat on a bench in the cemetery and made up for the time we'd lost being apart with kisses and making plans for our future. I was like a girl who had just got engaged. I was completely overwhelmed by the moment and the promise of my life with my one true love. I held and squeezed Alexander harder than I ever had before and became magically lost in his lips as I cherished that I was soon to become his vampire mate.

Waiting for an Eternity

I was going to become a vampire! It was all I'd ever thought about and dreamed about and now it was coming to fruition! I was so afraid I'd dreamed it that I texted Alexander a million times to reassure myself that it was real. It was, and it was going to be for all the right reasons.

What would I wear? Who would I invite? When would it happen?

The following evening, I met Alexander at the Mansion. As Stormy was eating, I sneaked a kiss with him upstairs in his attic room. "I'd like to invite Becky," I said.

"I figured you'd want to include the world."

"I do," I said. "Everyone I've ever met."

"You have to understand, many people might not want this to happen."

"You mean like Jagger and Luna?" I asked.

"Yes."

"They are not going to ruin my night!"

"They aren't going to ruin anything anymore," he said. "That's what he's told me. But I just wanted you to know . . ."

"That it's still hard to trust them?"

"I don't know . . ."

"Then we should probably keep this a secret," I suggested. "Make it private. It's the only way."

"I'm afraid you might be right," he said, caressing my hair.

"Is that how you imagined it? Just us?"

"No—but in this case, it might be for the best. If word gets out . . ."

"I know."

"Are you okay with that?" he wondered.

"I don't want anyone to stop this. And isn't it really between us?"

He nodded. "I want this to be a beautiful night for you."

"It will be. Just having you there. That's all I need."

"Yes," he said. "I'll be there. You can count on that."

But then I thought about the ceremony I'd always imagined. And it was missing someone who had been by my side since third grade.

For a moment I looked away. Alexander took my chin and drew me back to him. "What's wrong?"

"It's just that I really want Becky there—" I confessed.

He smiled. "I know."

"You do?"

"I think she should be there."

I gave him a huge hug. When we released our grip, he seemed as if he wanted to say something more.

"What is it?" I asked.

"I think Sebastian should be there as well."

Now a smile overcame my face. "Of course he should be there. I can't wait, Alexander. This is going to be wonderful."

He seemed equally excited.

"I'll set everything up," he said, gazing into my eyes. "The altar, the coffin, the ceremonial goblets."

"What can I bring?"

"Just yourself." He touched my cheek with the back of his hand. "I'd like you to come to the cemetery just after sunset," he continued. "I'll need some time to get ready for you and arrive myself."

"I won't be late," I said.

"And then we will finally be together—as we both have always imagined." He gave me a long, tender kiss that sent tingles down my spine.

"I'm going to find a dress," I said. "One that you'll remember for eternity. Did you tell Stormy?" I asked my boyfriend.

"I thought you'd want us to tell her together," he said.

I was so pleased with Alexander's sensitivity. Stormy had originally wanted Alexander to bond with Luna. But now that she saw Luna's true colors, she might be happy that I was the one who was going to the altar with her brother after all.

Alexander grabbed my hand and led me down the attic stairs, then the main ones. We found Stormy petting Phantom and reading a fashion mag in the parlor while Jameson was in the kitchen cleaning up from dinner.

Alexander sat down beside her and I sat on the other side of him.

"What's up?" she said. "Is something wrong?"

"No," Alexander said, putting his arm around her. "I just wanted to let you know—Raven and I are going to have a ceremony."

"What kind of ceremony?" she asked quizzically.

"The covenant kind," he replied.

Her eyes widened and she looked at me. "You are going to be turned?" She was as excited as she was surprised. "You really are going to do it?"

I nodded.

"This is so fabulous!" she said. "Can I come?"

"We'd like you to be there," Alexander said. "In fact, Raven wants to do this while you are here. That is why we are going ahead with it so soon."

"That is so sweet!" Stormy rose and gave Alexander a hug, then gave me a loving embrace. "Will Billy be my date?"

"Uh . . . no," Alexander said. "That's what we want to talk to you about. This is going to be private."

"Mother and Father won't be there?" she asked.

"We want to do this soon. There isn't time. We are also inviting Sebastian and Becky. But that's all. We don't want word to get out. You know how the Maxwells can be."

"I see that now. My lips are sealed," Stormy said. "I am

so happy you'll finally be like me."

I was so flattered that Stormy was so pleased. I couldn't wait to be part of their family.

"What will I wear?" she wondered.

"You can wear the dress you wore to the fall dance," I told her.

"What will you wear?" she asked me.

"I have only a short time to figure that out," I said. "But will you be the flower girl? We need someone to scatter the dead black roses."

"I'm your ghoul," she said with a wink.

And with that, we finished the evening with some smoothies, knowing in just a few more days, I'd be requiring the Romanian kind.

I looked at the world with almost vampire eyes as I awoke the next day and headed off to school. This was routine to me—drag myself out of bed, cower from the bright sun, take an all-too-short shower, get dressed in my brooding attire, and spend my day at school watching the clock until the final bell rang. In two days, however, I wouldn't be waking up in the daylight but going to bed just before it. I wouldn't be going to school and having to suffer through mundane subjects or lessons with teachers who favored the popular students. Instead, Jameson would tutor me one-on-one in subjects that interested me. I wouldn't have to take Trevor Mitchell's harassment anymore. Instead of seeing him, I'd be seeing Alexander.

As I breezed through the hallway, we passed the

Prada-bees, who stared at me with their usual contempt.

"Hi, Heather. Hi, Courtney," I said gleefully.

"Uh . . . hi, Raven."

"I like your purse," I said truthfully to Courtney, who was holding a bright blue designer satchel. "It matches your eyes."

"Uh . . . thanks, I guess."

When we turned the corner, I saw my nemesis slink down the corridor as if he were a teacher instead of a student.

"Hi, Trevor," I said when he got closer.

He looked at me skeptically. "Uh . . . hi. Did you have something you want to tell me?"

"No, just wanted to say hello."

"Well, that's very unlike you. You wouldn't be planning something sinister, would you?"

"No, something wonderful."

"Not egging my locker? Or keying my car?"

"No. Not those things at all."

I stretched my arms out and before he could retreat, I leaned in and gave my nemesis a long hug.

His body eventually melted into mine. It was bizarre to be standing in school hugging Trevor Mitchell. But I really meant it. There was warmth that flowed from me to him and vice versa. Though we had had our fights and tormented each other, I had known him since we were in kindergarten. Besides my family, it was the longest relationship I'd had in my life. And though it was mostly negative, I could always count on him being there for me—to judge, bother, and pester me. And through those years, I gave it back to him each time. And for a moment, in the middle of the hallway at Dullsville High, we came together as one.

I released our embrace and gazed up into his green, surprised eyes. Then I left him standing there watching me and wondering what had just happened as I walked to class.

For the first time since attending school, I really listened to my teachers. Some continued to be boring, but most were really passionate about the lessons. Maybe they had things to teach me all these years. And today, the teachers and their lectures really meant something to me, and after each class I went up to them and told them that, leaving each one shocked and confused.

"You've been acting funny all day. What is going on?" Becky asked when we got into her truck after school and I told her to drive to Evans Park.

"Swear to secrecy?" I asked her when we sat down on our favorite swings. "You can't tell anyone."

"I'll try." She appeared concerned.

"Alexander is going to turn me."

Becky gasped. "Are you kidding?"

"No. It's really going to happen."

"When?" she asked, still shocked.

"Tomorrow night."

"Then you will be—"

"What I've always wanted to be."

"But I thought you were going to wait. Until college," she said as the news sunk in.

"I promise nothing will change."

"What about school?" Becky was concerned.

"Alexander told me I can be homeschooled by Jameson. You can come over, too."

"But who will I eat lunch with?"

"Matt."

"I can't bear to be without you, Raven," she blurted out.

I wasn't sure how Becky would take the news, but I kind of knew it might be hard.

"Me too," I said, tears welling in my eyes.

"I'm happy for you but sad for me."

"Please don't think of it that way. You are so much more popular in school now. You are dating a jock. A handsome and nice one."

"But you've always been there."

"And I always will be. You can still drag me to games, and we can do our homework together at night. It's really only a few daylight hours that we'll miss."

"The ones that you missed with Alexander, now we'll miss."

"I'm not choosing him over you or anything like that," I said.

"I know. But we've been friends since third grade. It's just going to be a big change."

"I've seen you grow," I told my best friend. "You don't need me like you did."

"I always will. We're best friends."

"Yes, we are. That won't change. I want you to be there when it happens," I said. "I need you, too."

"Me?"

"Yes, you and Sebastian. You are the only ones we are inviting. And Stormy, of course."

Becky smiled as if she was pleased to be the one I was inviting and excited that she'd be there to share it, too. "This is scary—and amazing. I can't believe this will really be happening," she said.

"I know, me too."

"What do I do?" she asked worriedly. "What do I wear?"

"You can wear whatever you want," I said, trying to calm her down. "Whatever you feel comfortable in."

She began to spin, trying to think of outfits. "I have a new dress that I bought for fall."

"Whatever you want."

"But what happens at the ceremony?"

"Alexander and I will be at the altar. We'll stand by a coffin. There will be two goblets and some candles. He'll say some words in Romanian about our lives together, and then we'll drink from the cups."

"Okay . . . then what?"

"Then he'll bite me."

"Oh, geez," she said. "That's what I was afraid of."

"It will be okay, really." I took her hand.

"I know . . . but it's not something I'm used to. I'm used to seeing people kiss at the end of a ceremony."

We both laughed, her nervously and me with excitement.

"And then what happens?" she asked as I withdrew my hand.

"Hopefully, I'll be a vampire."

"Just like that?"

"I think so."

"Aren't you afraid?"

"Me? Afraid?" I said. "Just of *not* being one."

"It will be hard," she said, "but I'll be there."

We rose from our swings. She gave me a huge hug, and I knew then what I always had known since third grade— that I had the best friend on earth.

Dullsville had several stores to buy wedding, prom, and other special-occasion dresses but none that catered to cemetery covenant ceremonies. I had to think hard and fast on where to find one. I didn't have time to order one online or to find the fabric and make the perfect dress. One place came to my mind: Jack's Department Store. I'd shopped there before and last year had found a dress left over from Halloween to wear for the first dance Alexander and I attended together—the Snow Ball. I was hoping I'd get lucky again.

Becky drove me to Jack's and I did a quick tour of the junior department.

"Nothing suitable for the cemetery," I told Becky. She agreed.

"Halloween is over," the clerk said when I asked her about any costumes they might have in stock.

Becky was cowering behind me as I challenged the saleslady. "But don't you have anything left over? On clearance? In the back?" I was desperate.

She shrugged her shoulders. She obviously didn't want to put herself out. But then I saw Jack Patterson, the owner of the store. He held a special place in his heart for me since I helped him sneak into the Mansion for a high school initiation when he was a senior and I was twelve.

"Raven. How are you?" he asked with that same handsome smile he had when I helped him get inside the Mansion.

"I'm fine. How are you doing?"

"And Becky. It's great to see you, too."

"Thanks, Jack. It's so nice to see you."

Jack was Matt's uncle, and he was familiar with my best friend as well.

"So what brings you ladies here today?" he asked in a pleasant voice.

"A dress." I couldn't possibly tell him what I needed the dress for, only that I needed one. "I'm looking for a Halloween dress. I was hoping you had something left over. It's only been a few weeks."

He paused. "We had some in back last time I looked," he said. "Let's go check."

I felt like a ray of moonlight hit me. We followed him into the stockroom, and he searched through men's clothes and a few women's winter dresses.

"Ah yes," he said. "Is this what you are looking for?" He held up a Snow White dress.

"Well, not exactly." It was pretty but not what I had in mind. And I hadn't imagined puffy sleeves, and I didn't have time to dye the entire dress black.

"We have more," he said, showing us an area of unsold costumes. "Feel free to sift through."

As I smiled at Jack, I recalled that time when I'd helped

him sneak into the Mansion, as I'd done so many times myself, and how far I'd come since then. Not only was I dating the vampire who had since moved into the Mansion, but I was on my way to becoming one myself.

I'd assisted Jack with his mission and, unknowingly, he was doing the same for me.

I was hoping to find a dress here, like I had done before for a dance. But this one was for an even more important occasion, a truly magical night that would change everything—would change me. Jack didn't know this, but the next time I saw him, I might indeed be a vampire.

"Whatever you find," he said with a twinkle in his eye, "I know you'll look beautiful."

"Thank you so much," I said sincerely. I was truly touched by his compliment; it meant the world to me. I raced over and gave him a warm embrace.

Jack was paged from the front of the store and gave us a quick wink good-bye.

Becky and I whisked through the stacks of costumes, hoping one would fill my ultimate desired covenant dress and be the right size.

"How about this?" Becky pulled out a blood-red dress, but it was at least three sizes too big.

"That one is better. But I'll have to cut it off and take in most of it."

I perused a rack of hanging costumes. But one by one, each was something other than what I needed.

"What do you think of this one, then?" Becky asked excitedly. I looked up, hopeful. She held up a tattered, bloody

prom dress, one a ghost girl would wear. Perfect for Halloween but not for my idea of a covenant ceremony.

"I do think it's cool, but it's white and red. And I'm not
sure it's the right mood. Even for me," I lamented.

"I guess not."

"I don't know what I'm going to do," I said. I only had
one day.

Then I spotted a dress hanging alone at the end of the
rack.

I was deflated from not finding the perfect dress, but
I decided to check it out. The closer I got to it, the more
hopeful I became. I reached for it and held it out to the
light. It was an off-the-shoulder black lace dress, with pearl
buttons decorating the middle of the corset like dewdrops.
It came with black lace gloves and a small lace bolero.

"I love this," I said, melting.

"It's so you!"

"I could wear this if I get cold." I modeled the bolero.

"It's gorgeous," Becky cooed.

"I hope it fits," I said, holding it up to me.

"I'm sure it will."

"I'm not going to be able to eat, anyway," I told her.
"I'm too excited."

Becky examined it as I held it against me. It looked like
a perfect fit.

"That dress was waiting for you—just like Alexander,"
she said.

We both jumped up and down and squealed with
delight until a saleslady came in and told us to calm down.

I awoke with a start with bats fluttering in my stomach. It was the day of the covenant ceremony—the day I'd always dreamed of. I had barely slept the night before and I knew my eyelids must have been droopy. I splashed water on them to try to revive my face. I drank my coffee and paid pleasantries to my family. But I couldn't eat or focus on anything today. I was excited, anxious, and impatient, like a bride on her wedding day must feel.

I couldn't even call Alexander. I knew he was lying in his coffin—like I would be only a day from now. My life would finally be different.

I called Becky and she tried to calm my nerves. I paced and watched the clock. When would the sun set? Why was it taking so long? I decided to try to enjoy my last hours of sunlight and hung outside on our swing, soaking in my last few rays. But I was still preoccupied by the sun's slow descent. The minutes seemed like an eternity.

An hour later, I heard my mom call me from inside. I left the sun and came in.

My parents were leaving for a dinner with friends. They were gathering their coats from the hall closet. Before they headed out, I stopped them.

"Wait," I said. I rushed over and gave them each a hug. The next time they saw me, I'd be a vampire.

"Why are you acting so strangely?" my mom asked. "You've been preoccupied all day and hanging by yourself outside. It's not like you. Are you and Alexander okay?"

"We've never been better," I told her. "Truly."

"Then why all the affection?" my dad asked. "You must be up to something . . ."

"I just want to say how much I love you guys." I really looked at my parents, gazed into their eyes, and gave them a warm smile.

"Are you okay?" my dad asked. "Do you have a fever?"

"I'm perfect," I replied with a grin. "I've never felt happier in my life."

"Well, I'm glad you're so happy," my mom said, and gave me another hug. I hugged her back with all my might.

"I am, too," my dad remarked, and kissed me on the forehead.

I waved as my parents headed out the door. Once they had left for dinner, I began to get ready for my big night. I took an extra-long shower and lathered myself with the sweetest of scents. I dried my hair and did my best to rid it of any imperfections. I headed for my room and put on my dress. It would be the last time I could see my reflection, and I wanted to make the most of it. I laced up my corset bodice and fluffed up the flowing skirt. I wore dark tights and studded platform heels. I drew on my gloves and added an oversized skull ring and a silver thumb ring to my right hand. I layered my wrists with several rubber, leather, and dangling bracelets. I touched up my eyes with heavy liner and shadow. I painted my lips with black lipstick. I stared at my reflection. For the first time in my life, I really felt beautiful.

I pressed my lips to the corner of the mirror, leaving a dark kiss to remind me of who I was leaving behind and who I was going to become.

I was hurrying down the staircase when Billy came in from the family room.

"Why are you so dressed up?" he wondered.

"I thought you were going to Henry's," I said. I wasn't expecting to see my brother. I hope his questions weren't going to delay me.

"He's coming here," he said.

"I'm going out," I said.

"What are you up to? What's going on?" he asked.

"Nothing. I dress like this every day."

"Not that fancy. Where are you going dressed like that?" he asked skeptically.

"Why, the cemetery, of course."

As I reached the door, I stopped. I turned and gave my baby brother a huge squeeze.

"Get off," he said. "What's wrong with you?"

"Nothing's wrong. Everything is right. Finally," I said, "everything is right."

Alexander was going to take care of all the covenant altar amenities, and Becky and Stormy were going to meet me at the cemetery with a basket of black roses.

I was usually late to school, but for this I was early. Neither Becky's truck nor Alexander's Mercedes were parked at the cemetery yet.

I did my best to climb the fence and not snag any of the lace or seams of my dress. Once I was safely over, I breathed in the cool night air and took in my surroundings as if I were in the cemetery for the first time.

The tombstones seemed to be welcoming me, and the stars appeared to have an extra twinkle.

I felt a warmth come over me as if I was doing what I was meant to be doing my whole life. I'd waited for this moment since I was a little girl, so I took in the sights and sounds around me. It was quiet and eerie, and the crisp night air gave me an extra chill. I was loving it.

This was my night. Our night. And I felt like I couldn't get to the altar fast enough.

Glistening candles began to illuminate my way to Alexander's grandmother's monument, and my heart was beating in overdrive with excitement. Next to the statuesque monument was the enchanting covenant altar. It was spectacular. Dozens of candles lay in a circle around it. Ivy wound itself through the dark wrought-iron trestle. A black coffin lay underneath with a lit candelabra and two pewter goblets. I only needed Alexander.

And then I saw him: a dark-haired figure with his back toward me in the distance just behind one of the sides of the trestle. He must have been making the final touches for our ceremony. I raced over to him. I took a deep breath. This was the moment I'd waited for all my life.

When I reached Alexander, he turned around.

I gasped in horror. Green eyes were staring back at me. It couldn't be. Not tonight. Not *this* night.

Trevor Mitchell was as gothed up as I was. His normally model-blond hair was newly dyed jet black and was gelled up and spiky. Several silver-studded earrings flashed from his earlobes. His fingernails were painted black. And he wore a menacing grin.

He leaned on the trestle as if he owned the cemetery. "It's what you've always wanted, Monster Girl."

I was stunned. First of all, I was expecting Alexander. And second, not in my wildest imagination was I ever expecting to see Trevor Mitchell dressed this way.

Trevor was hot and seductive. Part of the attraction I had felt for him before had been that we were opposites. However, with him staring back at me while dressed like a gorgeous goth, it was hard for me to take my eyes off him.

But as attractive as he was, he wasn't the reason I was here.

"What are you doing here?" I asked. "Where is Alexander?"

"That isn't important now."

"You need to leave. Like now," I urged.

"I'm right where I need to be," he said.

"How did you know about this?" I asked.

"I have my sources."

I paused. Who could have told him? Becky, but she wasn't even here yet. Sebastian? Did he have loose lips after all? "You don't even know what this is about," I challenged him.

"I do," he said confidently. "It's about becoming a vampire."

"What?" I was even more shocked. And slightly frightened that Trevor knew why I was here.

He grinned down at me. "It's why Jagger took you up on the altar—and Luna did with Sebastian. It's about bonding with another for eternity. On sacred ground. And this place is sacred enough for a hundred humans to turn into vampires."

I was even more taken aback by his knowledge of the evening. "Who told you that?" I asked.

"I told you, I have my resources. Or, rather, vampires."

"Scarlet?" I wondered. She wasn't likely to tell. Or was she? "But she didn't even know about tonight."

"Look what I've done for you." He rolled up his black sleeve. It was a tattoo of a raven.

"It's permanent," he said. "And I'm hoping we'll be, too."

I stared at his tattoo. What was Trevor doing? And what was he suggesting?

"What are you doing here?" I yelled. "Trying to ruin my night?"

"No," he said. "Trying to make it last forever."

"I don't know what you're talking about!" I shouted. "You aren't even a vampire!"

Then his fangs flashed in the full moonlight.

I gasped again and stepped back. "No . . . this can't be! *You* can't be."

I was living a nightmare. Trevor Mitchell, my nemesis, a vampire? And we were standing together on sacred ground.

I picked up my dress and inched back. "Who turned you?" I asked, breathless.

"That doesn't matter now. It's time to be talking about us. You and me. And eternity."

"There is no you and me!" I stepped back again, but he drew closer.

"I think there is." He took my arm and pulled me in to him and laid a riveting kiss on me. I was shocked and, for a moment, lost in the embrace. I felt like I had more than a year ago when he kissed me on the lawn of the Mansion on Halloween and several times before. He knew how to kiss and make a girl feel happy against his lips, but it was hard to see into his soul—if he had one. Tonight I felt something even deeper. I really felt in his lips that there was something more to his feelings than trying to seduce the goth girl. I felt that he loved me.

I wanted him to leave. I had assumed the Maxwells might have disrupted our evening, but I'd forgotten about the bigger threat—Trevor Mitchell. Though he was attractive and we had a lifelong connection, I was angry and sad for him that he was spoiling my big night. On my end, I was kissing the Monster good-bye.

I pushed his face away from me.

It was the one night I'd thought I didn't need my garlic. I didn't have anything to defend myself but me. I had to get him off of me and escape this situation. I kicked him in the shins as hard as I could. They must have taken a beating over the years of playing soccer, because he winced in pain and drew back, though he kept a tight hold of my arm.

I bared my teeth and was ready to bite at his arm when I saw a commotion by the tomb.

"I thought you were waiting for me—" Becky said as she approached the altar with Matt at her side.

"I am! This is Trevor!" I yelled to her. "Not Alexander."

I heard her gasp. "No—it can't be!"

Stormy emerged, holding her black satin basket of flowers. "I told Alexander he couldn't trust that guy! What is he doing up there?"

"What is *he* doing here?" Vibrant red hair came out from the shadows by the tomb. Scarlet's angry face matched the color of her hair.

I was surprised to see Scarlet. It was one thing to see Matt, but Trevor and now Scarlet, too?

"This was supposed to be private," I mumbled. "What is going on?"

"Why is Trevor up there with you?" Scarlet asked me.

A surprised Sebastian stepped out, too, into the

moonlight along with Onyx.

"He's a vampire," I said to her, "and now he plans to turn me."

"No—" she said. "It's not true! Don't listen to him!"

Trevor gripped my arm even harder.

"Then if you didn't, who did?" I asked her.

Just then a pink-haired girl stepped out of the shadows.

"Luna!" I said. "You never quit, do you!"

She seemed shocked to see Trevor up at the altar, just as I was shocked to see everyone here at the cemetery.

"But I do!" she said. "I don't know what you're talking about. Why is Trevor here?"

Romeo had been holding her hand, but then he moved away. "You turned him?"

"Of course not!" She grabbed his hand and pulled him back to her. "I thought she was going to be here with Alexander."

Jagger and Valentine appeared, too, seemingly shocked by Trevor and me at the covenant altar.

Trevor continued to grip my arm. I didn't feel the physical pain of his grasp as much as the emotional one of him threatening to bite me.

"Well, he's a vampire now and thinks he's going to turn me!" I shouted to them.

"No—" Becky said. "She was waiting for Alexander!"

"You can't do that!" Sebastian yelled to Trevor.

"This got out of hand!" Becky said. "I'm sorry, Raven, I only told Matt about tonight."

"Well, word travels fast in a small town, Monster Girl," Trevor said, drawing me close to his side.

"Let go," I said to him, "or I'll be going for *your* jugular!"

Trevor looked at his new audience—who were only a few yards away. It was hard to make them out from the flickering lights surrounding us. But when our eyes adjusted, it was clear. Everyone was stunned and didn't know what to do. My nemesis was brimming with confidence and pride. Then he looked at me. "I'm going to prove to you and everyone else that it's me you really want."

Trevor grinned madly and showed his fangs. He leaned back, ready to bite my neck. I was ready to kick, punch, and scratch my way out when I saw, out of the corner of my eye, Jagger and Sebastian rushing toward us.

All of a sudden a force from behind me pushed through us, and Trevor was thrown a few yards away from me and was lying by a tombstone as I fell back on the ground.

I looked up when a strong hand reached out to me. On it was a familiar spider ring.

I was overcome with emotion. "Alexander!" I exclaimed.

He appeared out of the night, shined a brilliant smile, and took my hand. Alexander was as gorgeous as I'd ever seen him. His black hair flopped over his chocolate-colored eyes and hung down seductively. He was a magnetic presence in a dark silk suit, blood-red tie, and matching pocket handkerchief. He helped me to my feet and gazed at me in my dress.

He really examined me and lit up with delight. "You are breathtaking," he said. "I couldn't have imagined you any more beautiful than you are now."

I was so pleased with his reaction and stared up at the handsome vampire before me.

"Are you okay?" Alexander asked.

"I am now," I said, squeezing his hand.

"It was supposed to be just us," he said with a sweet smile as Jagger and Sebastian returned to the watching crowd.

"I know. I guess everyone found out. But there was one person who I didn't ever think would be here."

We both looked to Trevor, who had just gotten back on his feet.

"Don't even think about it—" Alexander said to him angrily. Then he looked at me with soft and engaging eyes. "I have had just about enough of other guys trying to turn you, Raven. There is only one vampire who will," he said confidently. "The one who you were always meant for—me."

I melted inside. Alexander was as dreamy as ever.

"I want to ask you one more time," he said, pulling me close. "Is this what you truly want?"

"Yes!" I assured him.

"It's not too late to turn back," he said.

"Don't even think about it."

He smiled an alluring smile. I could think of nothing else but being with him forever.

My hands began to shake, but Alexander took them in his and drew me closer still.

"No!" Trevor cried. "Don't!" He fell to his knees, his right hand opening, revealing two fake fangs.

Trevor hadn't been turned. I should have known. He was just trying to stop me from being with Alexander.

For a moment, I felt for my nemesis, who had tried to declare his love for me and prove to everyone that it was he whom I belonged with. But I didn't belong with him. And that kiss that we had just shared was, for me, a kiss good-bye.

I glanced at the crowd of friends all warmly watching me. Becky, with joyful tears in her eyes, leaning against a handsome Matt; Sebastian, with his arm around Onyx; Luna, holding hands with Romeo. Scarlet looked as happy for us as she was angry at Trevor. Jagger, whose elbow rested on Valentine's shoulder, gave us a friendly nod. Then I saw a familiar threesome: my brother, Billy, with his best friend, Henry, and a grinning, adorable Stormy.

Alexander nodded to his sister, and she and Becky came toward us. Stormy sprinkled the flowers around us and the coffin, and Becky fanned out my dress. Then they both stepped back.

Alexander said a few beautiful words in Romanian, and we both sipped from the goblet.

Then I gazed up at Alexander—my gothic prince, my knight of the night. My true love.

He looked into my eyes and I knew the time was right. This moment we both were ready. And we both beamed happily.

"I will love you for all of eternity," he said.

He gently brushed a few strands of hair away from my shoulder. Chills danced along my flesh from his touch. He smiled and drew me close, then leaned in to me. He slid his fangs against my neck ever so slowly, causing my heart to race in anticipation. Then, as if they were always meant to be there, his fangs gently pierced my neck. They slid into my flesh like a thousand kisses on wanton lips. It was as if he was breathing new life into my veins. I felt euphoria soar through my whole being. My skin tingled, my senses were heightened, my heart flooded with love. Then, when he drew my blood as his own, I could feel him breathe me into him. It was truly magical, like he was drinking in my soul. I couldn't have imagined such an amazing feeling and here it was, coursing through my every cell. We were finally one. I wasn't undead. In fact, I felt more alive than I ever had before.

I was electrified. I was filled with true love.

He smiled a brilliant smile and licked the remaining blood from his lips. I could smell it. It was sweet, like honey. And suddenly I craved his blood, as if in his veins flowed the most delicious nourishment.

He squeezed my hands affectionately, and he then leaned in to me again and we kissed for an eternity. We both were consumed with bliss.

As we drew apart, I realized I could hear noises that I hadn't detected before, the sounds of birds and bats far away. The moonlight was brighter than I remembered, and I could feel it dancing on my skin. And I could see through the night—dusk instead of complete darkness—trees and tombstones once out of view after sunset were now visible.

I slid my tongue gently along my teeth and I felt something I'd never felt before—two pointy fangs. I was overcome with joy.

Alexander and I were connected in a much deeper way than we ever had been. I was truly bonded to him, as if our two hearts beat in rhythm and our blood circulated in harmony. It was like being one. We embraced, and then he held me in his arms. I melted against him and gazed into his dreamy eyes as he joyously gazed back into mine, cherishing what he did for me—what he did for us.

We turned back to our friends and family, who appeared as happy for me as I was. I knew I was the same person—but I was transformed. I was now a vampire.

Once again I remembered the time my kindergarten teacher had asked me what I wanted to be when I grew up and I had told her emphatically, "A vampire." If only she could see me now.

This was the life I'd always wanted and the life I was thirsting to live. And I couldn't wait to begin it as a vampire in the Mansion on top of Benson Hill with my true love, my handsome and mysterious vampire, Alexander Sterling, for all of eternity.

Acknowledgments

I would like to thank my wonderful editor, Katherine Tegen, for guiding my career and for being so invaluable to me and the Vampire Kisses series.

My fabulous agent, Ellen Levine, for your insight and expertise.

My awesome editors, Sarah Shumway and Julie Lansky.

And my in-laws and friends for your support: Jerry, Hatsy, Hank, Wendy, Emily, Max, Linda, and Indigo.